Sexting THE BOSS

K.C. WELLS

This is a work of fiction. Names, characters, places, and incidents either are the product of the author's imagination or are used fictitiously, and any resemblance to actual persons, living or dead, business establishments, events, or locales is entirely coincidental.

Sexting The Boss
Copyright © 2020 by K.C. Wells
Cover Art by Meredith Russell

Cover content is being used for illustrative purposes only and any person depicted on the cover is a model.

The trademarked products mentioned in this book are the property of their respective owners, and are recognized as such.

All Rights Reserved. No part of this book may be reproduced or transmitted in any form or by any means, including electronic or mechanical, including photocopying, recording, or by any information storage and retrieval system without the written permission of the Publisher, except where permitted by law.

Chapter 1

Since when did it become so difficult to get laid on a Friday night? So what if I wasn't in the mood to go out? There had to be plenty of guys in my area who wanted some action, right?

Wrong. No one on Grindr was ticking my boxes. As a last resort, I'd called up Ste. I'd figured he was a safe bet. He says he's bi, and that amounts to turning up at my apartment whenever he wants to get fucked or suck a dick. Like I'd say no to that, right? But this was one of the few times I'd called him—and he was throwing me over for football.

"Aw, come on, Ste. You know you wanna."

"Maybe, maybe not. But there's football on TV, and…"

Football? Was he freaking *kidding* me? "And you're gonna pass on my dick for *football*?" I wasn't gonna back down. I had a severe case of blue balls, and that meant I was gonna fight dirty.

"I bet I could make you change your mind," I wheedled.

He snorted. "Not unless you're suggesting coming round to my place and letting me sit on your cock while I watch the game. Mind you, the rest of the guys would probably love it. We might end up being the half-time entertainment."

That did it. This was a challenge, and I was more than ready for it.

I unzipped my fly, shoved my jeans down to my knees, and pumped my already meaty dick a couple times. Had to get it looking its best for the camera, right? Then I grabbed it around the base, holding it erect while I got the camera ready. *Click.* I checked the photo, liking how my cock filled the frame, then hurriedly sent it to Ste, along with the message, 'Thinking of you.'

"Tell me you don't want a piece of that," I told Ste confidently, still lazily tugging on my shaft. Victory was mine. I could picture him drooling when he got the photo.

"Piece of what? You're not taking no for an answer tonight, are ya?"

Goddamn snail mail. "Just check your inbox. Sent you a little something."

Ste huffed. "Fine." I could hear the TV in the background. "Okay, what I am supposed to be looking at?"

"The photo I just sent you."

"Nope. No photo here. And before you ask, I just refreshed. Sorry, Chandler. Whatever you sent is out there somewhere in the ether. And now I'm gonna watch the game. Have a good night." Bastard was laughing as he disconnected.

I stared at my phone. If he didn't get it, then

who did?

Before I could fathom that out, my phone pinged. When I saw the email from Stu Ganford, I had to admit I was puzzled. Since when did I get emails from the boss on a Friday night? I opened it, and was no clearer.

Meeting in my office, Monday morning at 9.00.

Stu

Huh?

For one thing, it wasn't his usual format. Stu Ganford was a succinct man, I grant you, but one-line emails were not his style. Signing it Stu wasn't his style either.

What the fuck is going on?

I read it again, only this time a terrible idea began to dawn. Stu…. Ste…..

Oh God. Sweet Jesus, I didn't. Tell me I didn't.

I clicked through my sent messages, and Holy Mother of God, there it was.

I'd sent a dick pic to Stu Christ Almighty Ganford. Who now wanted to see me in a meeting.

I sagged into the couch, the phone dropped onto the seat cushion beside me. Well, that was it. Goodbye, job, Hello, unemployment. And I could kiss goodbye to any positive references. Employers who received explicit photos of staff genitalia tended not to write about them in glowing terms for future employers.

As if in response, my erection wilted, my balls shriveling. I was well and truly fucked.

It took me a moment to realize my phone was buzzing. I glanced at the screen apprehensively, in case Stu had decided he couldn't wait until Monday. Thankfully it was Dean, a coworker. I connected the call absently, my mind still on Stu's email. "Hey."

"I forgot to mention today that I'm having a BBQ Saturday, and you're welcome to come. I know it's a bit last minute and all."

Dean was an okay kinda guy. We chatted about sports and movies, he'd tell me how many girls he was banging, and I'd tell him how many guys I was screwing. Really symbiotic relationship.

Right then a BBQ was the last thing on my mind.

"Sorry, but I'll have to pass."

"Sure. Like I said, it's last minute, so I get it. You going out tonight with the rest of the gang? Rachel, Joey, Phoebe, Monica…?" He snickered, like he always did every goddamn time he said it.

I don't know which I hated more—my name, or the fact that everyone felt they had to make a joke out of it. So my mom loved Friends. So what? Except right then I was in no mood for Dean's laughter at my expense.

"I really don't need this. In fact, the joke is wearing pretty fucking thin."

I thought I heard Dean choking. A moment

later, he was back. "You okay, buddy?"

And just like that, I regretted my outburst. "Sorry, Dean. I... I got a lot on my mind."

"Wanna tell me about it? A problem shared, as they say."

I deliberated telling him for all of two seconds. I had no one else to talk to, for God's sake. "I... might have just sent Stu Ganford a photo of my cock."

Okay, this time he was definitely choking. "Jesus fucking Christ, Chandler!"

"It was an accident! I was sending it to someone else. Come on, don't tell me *you've* never done it. Because I've seen your phone, remember?"

"Sure, yeah, I've sent a girl a dick pic, but I'm always real careful when I'm sending."

"It was one letter different, that's all." One goddamn letter that was gonna cost me my job.

"Maybe he won't get the message. Maybe he won't see it."

Bless his optimistic little heart. "And *maybe* he already saw it, and emailed me to say he wants to see me Monday morning."

"Aw shit. Really? That's too bad."

"Too bad? You do realize he's gonna can me for this, don't you? Because once I step into that office come Monday, my ass is grass and he's a fucking lawnmower."

Dean sighed. "Looks like there's nothing you can do, except hope he's feeling lenient. You might get away with a reprimand."

"Yeah, and pigs might fly outta my butt." I'd had enough. I had a whole weekend to come of thinking about Monday, and I was already depressed as hell. "I'll see you Monday morning, okay? Until I get my marching orders."

"Try not to think like that. You don't know what's gonna happen."

Yes, I do, I thought as I disconnected the call. *And it's not gonna be pretty.*

"What do you mean, I can't see him?" This was driving me nuts. "He asked to see *me*, this morning."

"I know that," Fiona explained with more patience than I would've had in the circumstances. "But as I told you this morning—and on each of the…" She glanced at her notepad. "…four occasions you've asked to see him, Mr. Ganford is very busy. When he's ready to see you, he'll let you know." She went back to peering at her monitor.

There was nothing to do but go back to my desk and wait for another unspecified period of mental torture. I glanced at the clock on the wall in the hallway. It was already four in the afternoon. The office closed at five, for God's sake. Was he gonna keep me waiting until the end of business?

And then it hit me. Of course he was. It was his way of making me sweat.

Damn him. It was working.

I sat at my desk, trying to focus on my insurance reports. Like that was possible. When five o'clock came, people got up and headed out of the office, exchanging comments and wishing me a good evening. Dean said nothing as he strolled past, but he patted my shoulder twice. When I caught sight of Fiona walking toward the door, her purse over her shoulder, I sighed with relief.

He's gone. Then I realized I'd have to go through the whole process again the following day. If he hadn't been about to fire me, I'd have sued him for mental cruelty.

The irony of the situation was not lost on me. As bosses went, Stu was drop dead gorgeous. Short brown, neat hair, brown eyes, a permanent five o'clock shadow, and this sexy lopsided smile that always did things to my insides.

Okay, I'll admit it. My boss was hot.

"Chandler."

I glanced up and froze. Stu stood at his office door, his jacket and tie removed, the top two buttons of his pale blue shirt open. "Sir?"

He beckoned with his finger. "My office. Now." Then he disappeared behind his pale wooden door, leaving it ajar.

Fuck. This was it.

I shut down my computer, tidied my desk, picked up my jacket and bag, and trudged along to his office.

"Close the door."

I shut it behind me, and waited. Stu pointed to the empty chair facing his desk, and I hurriedly sat down. Disconcertingly, my knees were shaking. I put my jacket over them, then balanced my bag on top.

Stu walked over to his filing cabinet and opened the top drawer. To my surprise, he removed a bottle of whiskey and two glasses. He glanced over at me. "Drink?"

"I think I need one," I croaked.

Stu chuckled, before pouring two good measures. He handed me a glass, then sat in his big, wide chair. "Well, well, well. You certainly surprised me."

I said nothing, but sipped the whiskey. He probably had this whole speech worked out.

"I suppose you know why I sent for you."

I sighed. "Because I accidentally sent you a dick pic." There was no point being coy anymore.

Stu paused, his glass halfway to his mouth, his forehead creased in a frown. "Accidentally?"

Wait—what?

Before I could get my head around the implications, Stu put down his glass. "I see."

No, I wanted to yell. *You don't see*. Because I was just starting to figure it out. But some inner voice kept me quiet.

"Well, in that case…" Stu leaned back in his chair. "In ordinary circumstances, I would be informing you that your employment here was at an end."

I took a mouthful of whiskey before trusting myself to speak. "Ordinary circumstances?"

Stu smiled, and his eyes glittered. "As you might have realized by now, these are *not* ordinary circumstances. What I am about to propose will mean the continuation of your employment here—if you agree to my terms."

My breathing caught, and I put down my glass.

"I can see I have your full attention, so I'll come to the point and I'll be blunt. You get to keep your job, as long as I get to fuck you."

I blinked. He wants to…. I fought hard to maintain my self-control. *This is a dream, right? The kind of dream you never want to wake up from.*

I licked my suddenly dry lips. "You get to… fuck me?"

Stu nodded. "Whenever I want. Wherever I want." That smile hadn't dimmed. "I'm aware this amounts to blackmail, but I've done my homework when it comes to you, Chandler. I don't think what I'm proposing could be called rape, do you? That implies without consent, and I don't feel that would be an issue, do you?"

My first thought was that my boss knew me

a helluva lot better than I thought he did.

"I should add at this point that accepting this proposal will neither help nor hinder your possibilities for advancement in this company." Stu locked gazes with me. "You don't get to rise through the company just because we're fucking. Any advancement would be purely on merit."

God, every time he said 'fucking', my brain did a default to an image of me spread out on his desk, while he plowed into me.

I struggled to keep my mind on topic. "You... you could have anyone you want. There have to be hundreds of guys out there who'd be willing to bend over for you." And I was one of them. In a heartbeat.

"But I don't want 'hundreds of guys', he air-quoted. "I want you. On tap, as it were. At my beck and call. These are dangerous times we live in, as I'm sure you can appreciate. I never know if the person on a screen is the one who'll turn up at my door. I prefer to take risk out of the equation. You're a known quantity. You're gay. And you like sex." He grinned. "You wouldn't believe the conversations that reach my ears. And apart from that, I have you over a barrel." His eyes shone. "I'd rather have you over my desk. Or over the back of that couch over there."

"I don't have a choice, do I?" Not that I wanted one. There was no way I was about to tell him he was offering me all my dirty fantasies on a plate. *Let him think he has the upper hand.*

"Is that a yes?" Stu got up from his desk, walked around it, and came to a halt beside my chair. He cupped my chin, tilting it until I was staring up at him. "If you'd rather not do this, then we'll call it a day and you can leave when you've worked off your notice. I'll even give you a reference."

The last part took me by surprise. I definitely hadn't expected *that*.

I gazed at his lips, so pink and full, and damn it, I was imagining them around my cock. My heart hammered. I didn't want to leave. And I wanted him.

Quick mental calculation. *I get to keep my job, and get fucked by my hot AF boss.*

No-brainer.

"You do know this is illegal, right?" One last attempt not to appear *too* eager.

Stu's eyes gleamed. "You have no proof of this conversation. There's no one around to overhear us. Hence that barrel I have you over." His fingers caressed my cheek. "It won't be an onerous task, I promise. And I'm not exactly unskilled. Put it this way. I've never had any complaints." He bent over and whispered into my ear, "Not that you're in a position to complain anyway."

Fuck, he smelled amazing. And okay, I'll be honest. Right then he got me wondering about his skills. Especially with his tongue…

Whoa boy. I had to rein in my libido. Drooling was not exactly a sign of reluctance.

Stu straightened and regarded me steadily. "Well? What is your answer?"

I took a deep breath. "I accept your terms." Which was a damn sight milder than me clearing his desk with a sweep of my arm, bending over it and dropping trou.

Stu's smile widened. "Excellent. Then I see no point in wasting time, do you?" He let go of my chin and slowly undid his belt.

I glanced down, my heartbeat climbing even more when I got a glimpse of his bulge.

This was gonna be a stretch. Then a thought occurred, and me being me, I couldn't keep my mouth shut. "Just one last question. I get to fuck you too, right?"

Chapter 2

Stu
Wait—what?

For a moment I was stunned into silence. This wasn't the way things were supposed to go. Because up until him dropping that question so casually into the conversation, it had been proceeding exactly as I'd imagined. Better yet, if I read Chandler's reactions correctly, he wasn't totally averse to my proposal.

Like I hadn't known that all along. The guy was a total slut. The times I'd caught snippets of conversation between him and Dean, sharing tidbits about their sex lives, and it had become clear Chandler liked guys. A lot. And then that text...

Okay, so I'd really thought he was making a move on me. Unexpected? Sure. Unwelcome? Hell no. But when it turned out to be a mistake, I had to think fast. Because *no way* was I going to lose out on that tasty piece of arse. Chandler was cute, with brown eyes, glasses, and a thick shock of hair on top. God, how many times had I fantasized about fucking him over my desk, tugging on that hair, hearing him beg for my cock?

"Do I take silence for consent?"

I blinked. Chandler was gazing up at me—and smirking.

I responded the only way I could think of. I laughed.

Chandler arched his eyebrows. "And that's not an answer." He grinned.

Okay, he was way too smug for my liking. "It would take an exceptional man to make *me* bend over for him." *Go on. Read into that what you will.*

Chandler's eyes gleamed. "Game on then."

I frowned. "Excuse me? What did I just say?" Christ, he was taking it as a challenge. *He truly imagines getting his cock in my arse.*

Disconcertingly, my dick twitched, and fuck me, he noticed.

"Well, it wasn't a yes. It wasn't a no either." That grin hadn't diminished. "I'm good with a solid maybe."

How the hell did this happen? One minute I had control of the situation, the next, it was slipping through my fingers, and Chandler had the upper hand.

Chandler's gaze flickered down to my crotch. "So, what's next?"

No way was I walking out of that office without satisfaction. "I believe I was in the middle of what's next when you sprang that question on me." I slowly unzipped my fly and stroked my aching cock through my briefs. "So how about you put that mouth to some good use?" I pointed to the floor. "On your knees."

Chandler slid off the chair and lowered himself to the floor in one graceful movement. He sat back on his haunches, staring at my crotch and licking his lips.

Dear God, let him be good at this.

Then I smiled to myself. *Was* there such a thing as a crap blow job?

"Take it out then." I grinned. "It's not going to blow itself."

Chandler grasped the waistband of my pants and pulled them down over my hips, leaving my briefs in place. His eyes widened, and my chest swelled with pride.

Yeah, I was big, and I knew it. On occasion, *too* big for some guys. But judging by the light in Chandler's eyes, he was a size queen, so maybe there was hope.

Chandler inched closer, his nose rubbing along my shaft, like he was a connoisseur appreciating a fat cigar. Oh yeah. This was going to be good.

Slowly, reverently even, he lowered my briefs, and my cock sprang up, smacking against my belly. That hitch in Chandler's breathing was delicious.

"Oh fuck, you're uncut."

That got me curious. "And is that a good

thing or a bad thing?"

I swear he was drooling. "Oh, definitely good." He curled his hand around the shaft and gave it a couple of tugs, the head sliding out from beneath the foreskin. "Well, hello there."

Any scathing remarks I was about to make about treating my dick as if it was a person, died in my throat as he took the head into his mouth and gave it a hard suck. Then he slid a little more between his lips, his hand working the shaft.

Scrap any doubts I'd had. Chandler was born to suck cock.

I unbuttoned my shirt from the bottom up, thankful I'd already removed my tie. Chandler took the hint and reached up to stroke my belly, aiming for my chest. When he teased my nipple, it felt like an electric shock jolted through me, all the way to my balls. Chandler's appreciative noises as he swallowed more and more of my dick were doing wonders for my ego, and I cupped the back of his head, encouraging him to go a little faster.

Fuck. He was halfway along my cock, bobbing like a piston, and I was in heaven. I grabbed his hair, yanking him back, then smacked my cock against his cheek, before plunging it beneath his lips once more. I repeated the action three or four times, occasionally smacking my dick on his tongue. Then it was back to him bobbing on my cock while he worked the shaft, accompanied by a constant flow of appreciative moans.

Until I wanted more.

Tired of holding back my shirt, I removed it altogether, dropping it to the floor. I placed both hands on his head and held him steady while I fucked that talented mouth faster and faster, never pushing my cock too deep.

Chandler groaned, shoving my pants down to my knees, before grabbing my hips to anchor himself.

"How much can you take?"

He pulled free and looked up at me, his eyes shining. "As much as you've got."

I laughed. "Then put your money where your mouth is."

Chandler gazed at my solid dick, breathed deeply, then slowly took me into his mouth, until his nose was buried in my pubes and his face was red.

Oh my fucking God. My cock was surrounded by wet heat. Then he pulled back, spluttering, saliva dripping from my dick. He looked up, grinning. "Just so you know? I'm gonna have a sore throat tomorrow." Then he did it again, and I groaned from the exquisite pleasure of it all. When he pulled free again, red-faced and choking a little, I took pity on him. I pulled my cock upright, holding it against my belly.

"Suck my balls."

Chandler licked a line up my dick, then all the way down to my sac, dragging the soft skin with his tongue. He flicked it against my balls, tonguing them and sending shudders through me. When he stopped, I wanted to growl in frustration.

"Pants off," he said breathlessly.

I was too far lost in a haze of lust to deny him. I toed off my shoes, and Chandler pulled my pants down to my ankles, helping me to step out of them. Then he tugged me forward, until he was sitting on the floor between my spread legs, his mouth poised under my sac.

"Now jerk yourself off," he instructed, before taking one ball into his warm, wet mouth.

If I'd thought I was in heaven before that…

I tugged on my shaft while he sucked on my balls, taking one, then the other into his mouth, the movement of my dick smacking them against his tongue.

It was too much.

With a low cry, I shot my load, the cum pulsing out in an arc and spattering the carpet. Chandler reacted instantly, taking my cock into his mouth and sucking on it, while I shuddered through my climax, holding onto Chandler's head to steady myself. When he came to a stop, with one last lick along my softening shaft, I sighed heavily.

Chandler peered up at me. "So we're good? You get to fuck me, and I get to keep my job?"

I gazed down at him. "We're good. Just as long as you're prepared." I smiled.

"And what does that mean?"

"It means," I said as I stepped back and retrieved my briefs, pants and shirt, "you need to ready for any eventuality."

"Not sure I like the sound of that." He eyed me with suspicion.

I snorted. "Doesn't matter whether you like it or not, does it?" I had plans for that mouth. Not to mention that arse.

Chandler got to his feet. "Are we done?"

"For now." Then I reconsidered. "You're good at sucking dick." Praise where praise was due, after all.

He stilled. "I did a good job?"

Better than good, I thought, but I wasn't about to let him get a swollen head. "Let's say, you've set the bar high. Now you have to maintain your standards." I zipped up my fly and fastened my belt, my shirt back in place. Then I glanced at my watch. "Time you were out of here."

Chandler nodded. He picked up his bag and jacket, and headed for the door.

On impulse, I called out to him. "See you in the morning." I smiled.

I'd obviously done the right thing. He returned my smile. "See you then."

When I was sure he'd left the building, I sank into my chair. He'd derailed me with the whole 'accidentally' line, but it was still win-win as far as I was concerned. I now had a whole series of office encounters to look forward to. And who said it had to stay in the office?

What came to mind was Chandler's question. '*I get to fuck you too, right?*'

It had been a long time since I'd bottomed. And I hadn't lied. It would take someone exceptional to get me to take their dick. Except that after that stellar blow job, Chandler was showing signs of being more exceptional than I'd given him credit for.

The future was looking very promising indeed.

"Goodnight, Mr. Ganford," Fiona said, poking her head around my door. "Have a good evening."

"You too." I peered at my watch. "Has everyone left?" It was past five-thirty, and generally staff didn't hang around long.

"Dean's just gone, and Chandler's still at his desk."

"Is he?" I asked innocently. Like I hadn't asked him to stay behind again. Two days since our first meeting, and I wanted more. Only this time, I was going to make things interesting. "Don't worry about Chandler," I said with a wave of my hand. "I'll be going soon myself."

"Okay then." One last cheerful smile, and

she was gone, closing the door behind her. I got up and stood by the window, staring down into the street below. *There she goes, off to catch her bus.* I walked to my door, opened it and called out, "In here, Chandler." Then I retook my seat at my desk.

Moments later, he appeared, looking smart in a dark blue waistcoat and pants. He shut the door. "So what's it going to be tonight? Because I'm guessing you asked me to stay late for one reason only."

"You're going to fulfil a little fantasy for me." I grinned, before stroking my wide, tidy desk. "Beautiful, isn't it?"

He sighed. "Aha. So it's *fuck me on the desk* time, is it?"

"Not exactly." I beckoned with my finger, and he walked slowly around to where I was sitting, a faint frown creasing his brow. As he got closer, my nostrils caught a warm, earthy scent. "Are you wearing cologne?" It was perfect for him. It was also stirring my senses.

"Yeah. Is that okay, or is there a rule about not wearing cologne that I wasn't aware of?"

"It's fine." I cocked my head to one side. "You don't usually wear it, that's all."

I couldn't miss the flush that crept up his neck. "Well, today I did."

The thought wouldn't go away. *Did he wear it for me? Interesting.*

Chandler coughed. "Now, about this fantasy

of yours…. What did you have in mind?"

I pushed back my chair and pointed to the gap beneath my desk. "I want you to get under there."

He blinked. "Why?"

"Because one of these days, I want you under my desk, sucking my cock, while Fiona comes and goes. I want to know if you're up to the challenge."

His eyebrows shot up. "You want me… to suck you off… while someone else is in the room?"

I chuckled. "If you don't think you're up to it… I mean, it would require real skill. Because one sound from you, and the cat would be out of the bag."

Chandler snickered. "And who says *you* can keep a straight face while I blow you?"

I huffed. "I think you're overestimating your skills."

He shook his head slowly. "Not gonna happen. And do you know why? Because if either of us gave the game away, you'd come off worse. A boss, letting his employee blow him during office hours?"

I sighed. He was right, of course. "Okay. So I wouldn't do it. It was just something I saw in a film once. I thought it would be fun to suggest it, and watch your face."

To my surprise, Chandler wasn't laughing. Instead, he climbed under my desk and gazed at me expectantly. "Well, why don't we give it a try? You can pretend Fiona is right outside that door. We both have to be quiet as mice." He gave me a cheeky grin. "Nothing wrong with a little fantasizing."

Chandler was turning out to be more surprising by the minute.

He cleared his throat. "For this to work, you have to be within blowing distance."

I chuckled, and shuffled my chair forward. "This feels weird."

It was also turning me on.

I peered down. "You got enough space down there?"

He laughed, the sound echoing a little. Warm hands caressed my thighs, moving higher, until his fingers were on my belt. "As long as I don't get too enthusiastic, we're good." He lowered my zipper, tantalizingly slowly, and suddenly he was tugging at my pants, pulling them down. Chandler chuckled. "Oh. You *really* like this idea, don't you?"

I was hard as a rock.

Warm fingers curled around my dick, and I could feel his breath on the head. Fuck, that felt—

The door opened, and I froze.

Who the hell is that?

Chapter 3

Stu

"Mr. Ganford?" Dean popped his head around the door. "Sorry to disturb you when you're obviously still working."

"Mr. Porter. I thought you'd gone home." My heart was pounding. Beneath the desk, Chandler seemed to have frozen, thank God. "And yes, I'm still working." *So go away. Now.*

To my horror, Dean came into the office. "Actually, I'm glad of the opportunity to get you alone." He closed the door behind him, before approaching my desk.

The urge to scream *fuck off* was tremendous.

"Can't this wait until tomorrow?" Chandler's breath wafted over the head of my dick, and for one awful moment, I thought he was going to carry out his—my—fantasy. When nothing else happened, I breathed more easily.

"Getting in to see you these days is almost impossible." Dean grinned. "Fiona can be a pit bull when it comes to you."

I raised my eyebrows. "You'd better not let

her hear that description. You might find yourself on the receiving end of a complaint. And for your information, getting in to see me is as simple as sending an email. Fiona simply separates the wheat from the chaff. If she thinks someone else can solve an issue, then they get to deal with it, not me."

Whatever else I was going to say died in my throat when a hot, wet mouth encased the head of my dick. *Oh my God, he isn't going to—*

That thought was made redundant when Chandler swallowed my cock to the root without a fucking sound.

I exploded into a loud cough, and Dean frowned. "Are you all right?"

I wiped my mouth on my handkerchief. "I'm fine. Okay, do we really have to do this now? Because *you* may not want to go home, but I certainly do." Keeping an even tone and a straight face was the most difficult task I'd ever faced, because that tightness around my dick was exquisite. I wanted to pump into his mouth, to thrust deep, to fucking *move*, but of course I couldn't. And when Chandler began to slide my cock in and out of his mouth, sucking hard on the downward stroke, his fingers softly stroking my balls, I had to take my self-control to the next level. "So, can this wait?" God, how I kept my voice from cracking, I will never know.

"I wanted to ask you why I didn't get that

promotion last month."

Oh, for God's sake. Here *I* was, trying not to give it away that there was a man under my desk, bringing me closer to what promised to be the most explosive orgasm in the history of orgasms, and Dean wanted to—

Fuck. How did he do that without making a single sound? Not so much as a slurp.

I took a deep breath, not that it did any good. Chandler's soft fingers were stroking my shaft, sending electricity skittering along its length, deep into my sac, and zipping up my spine. He was close to making me come, and I was certain he knew it, the bastard.

"I believe I told you at the time," I enunciated carefully. "There were three candidates for the position. The successful candidate had more experience than you."

"Bullshit." Dean scowled. "Laura has been working in this office as long as I have. Christ, she even joined the company after me."

This was not happening. I opened my mouth to retort, but Chandler flicked his tongue over my frenulum, and I had trouble sitting still.

I am so going to kill him when Dean leaves.

Sounding a hell of a lot calmer than I felt, I clasped my hands on the desk. "That is true, but she came to us with five years' experience working in another—" Chandler gave my dick an extra hard suck, and I bit the inside of my cheek in an effort not to cry out. I cleared my throat. "Another successful copy-writing company. She had a proven track record. Were you not aware of her previous positions?" Chandler traced the length of my cock with his tongue, before giving it another good suck, and I squirmed in my chair.

"Oh." Dean appeared crestfallen.

"I'll take that as a no. So you'll admit she does have more experience?" I wanted to grab Chandler's head and skull-fuck him till I shot my load down his throat, but I needed to hold on a little bit longer.

"Yeah." Dean's tone said it all. "I'm sorry. I should have looked into it more before shooting my mouth off."

I was *this close* to shooting my spunk and I didn't trust myself to speak.

He sighed. "My apologies. I'll leave you alone." His brows knitted. "By the way, did you see Chandler leave? I was waiting for him to exit the building, but I couldn't see him."

I gave a quick shrug, all the movement I was capable of at that moment. "I assumed he'd left with everyone else." That last word came out as a croak as Chandler took me deep again.

"I must've missed him. I'll say goodnight then." Dean headed for the door.

"Goodnight, Mr. Porter. Have a pleasant evening." I pasted on a polite smile, fighting the rampant urge to thrust.

Dean paused at the door. "By the way. You might want to take something. It sounds like you're coming down with a cough or a sore throat."

"I'll take that under advisement," I assured him. Dean left, closing the door behind him. I waited for what I felt was a decent interval before reaching under the desk, grabbing Chandler's head and pulling him down onto my dick. "Now you're going to swallow every fucking drop," I gritted out, my hips finally in motion, bumping the head of my dick against the back of his throat.

Chandler spluttered, but I didn't give a shit. This was payback. I leaned back, hips pumping, eyes shut as I slid my cock into his mouth in a series of short, fast thrusts, relishing the noises that poured from his lips. I was going to enjoy every second of what was going to be an epic cum. And when that familiar jolt of pleasure crashed into me, I sat bolt upright, gasping, overwhelmed by the sensations. I thrust deep, one hand on his throat to feel it working as he swallowed, his own low moan mingling with mine.

When I was done, I sagged into the chair and pushed back, revealing Chandler's reddened face and swollen lips. I grinned. "Now *that* was something." I crooked my finger. "Get up. I'm not done with you."

He crawled out of the space, moving carefully so as not to bang his head. As soon as he was upright, I ignored my still half-hard dick and grabbed him, spinning him around until he faced the desk. Then I shoved him over it. "Grip the far edge and hold on. Don't let go."

"Hey. Don't tell me you didn't enjoy it." Chandler sounded surprised.

"Oh, I did. But this is for sucking me off while Dean was here." I reached around his waist and unbuttoned his waistband, then tugged his zipper down.

"That was *your* idea, remember?" he retorted.

"Yes, it was. My idea. And *my* decision if or when it happened, not yours." I grasped his pants and pulled them roughly to his knees, taking his boxers with them. There it was, the arse I'd been imagining, firm and round, a light dusting of hair over his cheeks, thicker in his crack. "God, that's a pretty arse." I grabbed both cheeks and spread him, revealing his hole, that tight little pucker that I was about to breach.

Chandler's breathing sped up. "Condom?"

I laughed. "Who says you're about to get fucked? That's wishful thinking, I'm afraid. Besides, that's probably just what you want right now, so I don't intend to give you that satisfaction." I leaned over him, whispering into his ear. "My terms, Chandler. *I* call the shots. *I* decide when it happens. Not you." And with that, I sucked on a couple of fingers, got them nice and wet, then slowly slid them into that warm, tight hole.

Not that I intended staying slow, but I wasn't a sadist. I could be gentle—for a minute. The heartfelt groan that rolled out of him told him he was feeling every inch of those fingers.

"There was a reason I never learned to play the piano," I whispered. "Fat fingers. They're a curse." That got me an even louder groan, and I snickered. "What's the matter? Feeling a little stretched?" I seesawed them in and out of him, not bothering any longer to take it easy on him. "God, you're tight. And your hole is clinging to my fingers." I glanced down at his cock, stiff against the edge of the desk, leaking pre-cum that descended in a long, glistening strand. "Oh, you like this." I gave his dick a light smack, and he let out a yelp. I sped up my finger-fucking, only now I took hold of his shaft and gave it a few good tugs.

"Stu…" It was almost a plea.

"Want me to stop? Because you *know* that's not going to happen. Or do you want more?" I withdrew my fingers, spat on them, then returned them, adding a third finger.

Oh my God, the sounds he makes.

I loved it when a guy was vocal. And right then, Chandler was letting me know in no uncertain terms that he fucking *loved* what I was doing. I forgot about punishing him, instead bending down to bite gently on that firm arse while I slid my fingers as deep as they would go. "Like it when I stretch you?"

"Fuck, yeah," he moaned softly. "Gonna make me come."

I sped up my movements. "That *is* the intention." I'd planned on edging him for as long as possible as retribution, but somewhere along the line, I'd changed my mind. I wanted to make him come. I wanted to feel the tremors coursing through him.

I didn't have to wait long.

"Can't wait to fill you with my cock," I said quietly, crooking my fingers inside him, his low cries telling me exactly when they found his prostate. "Think you can take it? Think you can sit all the way down on it?"

"Watch me," he gasped, his back arching slightly as I filled him. "Aw, fuck."

I chuckled. "Not tonight. I'm saving that for another time." I fucked him faster, his moans increasing in frequency and volume. "Quieter. You'll have the security guard wondering what the hell is going on in here." An outright lie—the night security team wasn't due for another half hour—but he wasn't to know that.

Then it was over, and Chandler's spunk was decorating the mat under my chair as his body tightened around my fingers. I milked his cock, gently squeezing until the last drop had left it. His breathing was harsh, his body trembling.

A satisfying conclusion, I had to admit.

At last his hole released me, and I withdrew

my fingers. I plucked a paper tissue from the box I kept behind my desk, and wiped them clean. Chandler hadn't moved, his fingers still gripping the edge of the desk as though holding on for fear of falling.

I caressed his arse cheek. "Can you stand?" My initial astonishment at his action had given way to a totally different emotion. I'd enjoyed watching his climax, proud of my part in it, and I wanted to know if he'd gotten as much out of it as I had.

Why his opinion should matter that much, I wasn't quite sure. This entire arrangement was for my benefit, not his, after all.

Except now? Something had changed, and I wasn't sure what.

Chandler stood, reaching down for his boxers and pants. I let him, dressing myself at the same time. My dick hadn't gone soft for a second, and I knew I'd be doing something about that when I reached my apartment.

I also knew who I'd be thinking about while I did so.

His clothing back in place, Chandler turned to face me. "Are we done?"

That wasn't the reaction I'd hoped for.

I nodded. And because I couldn't help myself, I added, "It felt good."

He blinked, and that look in his eyes was warmer. "Yeah, it did." He headed to the chair where he'd left his bag and jacket. "I'd better get out of here before the guard arrives." He sniffed the air. "And you may want to use an air freshener before he does. Smells like there was fucking going on in here." He grinned.

My gaze flickered down to the mat where the evidence still lay. "I suppose you expect me to clean this up."

He snickered. "It's your fault. Seems only fair. I didn't leave any trace of yours, now, did I?" And before I could utter another word, he was gone, leaving only the "goodnight" he called out as he left the office.

With a sigh, I grabbed a couple of tissues and wiped up his cum, before wadding them and dropping them into the trash. As an afterthought, I went into my private bathroom and picked up the can of air freshener.

I didn't want the cleaning staff knowing either.

Dinner was over, the dishwasher was already rumbling away, and I was shutting down my laptop for the night. It was like every other night, nothing out of the ordinary…

Except it didn't feel like that. Something was niggling at me, and I had no clue what it was. I glanced around at my apartment. Everything was as it should have been, yet…

"What the hell is wrong with you?" I said out loud. The TV was on, but it had only been a source of background noise. There was nothing I wanted to watch, but I still picked up the remote and clicked aimlessly. Then I tossed it aside and grabbed my phone, scrolling through news items, emails, and messages.

This vague feeling of dissatisfaction was starting to piss me off.

This is Chandler's fault.

That thought made no sense. How could it be his fault? I'd gotten off, hadn't I? Two blow jobs in three days, which was pretty good in my book.

That was when it hit me.

When was the last time a guy sucked me off?

When was the last time I had a guy in my bed?

I hadn't lied to Chandler that first time. There were crazies out there, and I had no wish to bring one into my home. Wasn't that why this whole situation existed? Chandler was the safe bet. I didn't want to bring *anyone* home.

Except 'home' was feeling like nothing more than a box to keep stuff in. That was all I had to show for my life so far. Stuff.

Only now, I was starting to realize that stuff wasn't enough. Not nearly enough.

My phone was still in my hand, and before I had time to think about it, I'd scrolled through my contacts and pulled up Chandler's number. I paused, my thumb poised above his number.

What am I doing?

I shrugged. *Fuck knows.* I hit Call and waited, my heartbeat speeding up a little.

"Hi." A pause. "Is something wrong?"

Maybe it was because he sounded… different somehow. Less sure of himself. I don't know. I just heard my own voice sounding equally unsure.

"Can we talk?"

Chapter 4

Stu

The silence that followed was almost tangible. "Talk?"

I laughed. "You know, a conversation? I say something, you respond, and so on?"

Another pause. "I *am* aware of the concept. I'm just a little surprised, that's all."

"Let me guess. You'd feel more comfortable if I called you up for phone sex?"

Chandler snickered. "Maybe not comfortable, exactly, but that would definitely be more what I've come to expect from you. After this past week, at any rate."

"There's more to life than sex." This time I paused. "Or does that not tally with your philosophy?"

Chandler's laugh filled my ears. "This from the man who's had two blow jobs from me in the past three days."

I had no idea where my next words came from, and they were out of my mouth before I had time to think. "Come over for a drink."

Silence.

"Chandler?"

"You're serious."

"I'm not in the habit of issuing requests I don't mean. And when I say a drink, I mean just that. That was *not* a euphemism for fucking." I wanted to lay my cards on the table before we went any further.

"A drink… and a conversation."

"Is the idea that fucking alien to you?" I was starting to rethink the whole stupid suggestion when Chandler finally spoke.

"Give me your address. And if we're drinking, I'll take a taxi."

About fucking time. I rattled off the address. "I'll see you when you get here." Then I disconnected.

What the fuck was that about?

I had no idea. I only knew I had to change something, and inviting him was the most radical change I could think of.

I took a quick look around the apartment. Nothing out of place, everything dusted and clean and sparkling, just like it always was. *Yeah. Untouched by human hands, except for mine.*

Well, that was about to change.

Half an hour later, the doorbell rang, and I

opened the door. Chandler stood there, dressed in jeans and a button-down shirt, his jacket slung over one shoulder. And yet again a warm, earthy scent clung to him, the same one from the office.

I had to admit, it really suited him.

"Hey, come on in."

Chandler stepped inside, and I closed and locked the door. He waited for me to lead the way, and I went into the living room. "You're okay with Scotch, right?"

"Scotch is good. With ice, please." He glanced around the room, saying nothing more.

I gestured to the couch. "Take a seat." Then I went over to the bar and poured two drinks, adding ice to his. When I turned, he'd sat at one end of the couch, his jacket draped over the arm, his body language a little stiff. I got that. This had to be totally out of his comfort zone. Drinks at the boss's house?

I handed him a glass, before taking the other end of the couch.

Chandler did another slow perusal of the room. "So, have you recently moved in?"

I took it the way it was intended, a comment on the lack of accessories on view. I knew how the apartment looked. No photos, no prints, no paintings. Not much in the way of furniture. What can I say? I like minimalism.

"That's your opening foray into conversation? We're going to discuss décor?"

Chandler's eyes sparkled. "I'd rather discuss you. Specifically, that accent."

"Ah, so you noticed that?" I smirked. "I always had you down as observant."

"How long have you lived in the States? Because I'm assuming you weren't born here, talking like that."

I sipped my Scotch, relishing its warmth. "We moved here from the UK when I was eleven."

"We?"

"My parents, my nine-year-old sister, and me. We went to live in Florida, because my parents started a business there. They still live there."

"But you don't." Chandler relaxed a little against the seat cushions. "Florida is a long way from Boston. Why here?"

"I went to college here. Once I graduated, I went into business. I saw no reason to move back."

Chandler smiled. "Well, you certainly haven't lost the accent. Don't you miss the weather? I should think it's a damn sight warmer in Florida."

It was my turn to smile. "Says the man who turned up in a shirt."

Chandler grinned. "Yeah, but I wore the jacket in the taxi. Shirt looks better, and you know how important it is to make a good first impression."

I couldn't help myself. "That cologne of yours says more than your clothes."

His eyes lit up. "That's the second time you've mentioned that. Anyone would think you like the way I smell."

Parts of my anatomy definitely did.

I steered the conversation back to safer ground. "Actually? This is closer to the weather I remember as a kid, before we moved over here." I drank a little, feeling more at ease. This was going better than I'd expected—except I wasn't sure *what* I'd expected. I didn't mind the small talk.

"Did you mean what you said? About being afraid to meet guys online or via apps?"

And there it was, the shift I'd anticipated, only later than I'd thought.

"I wouldn't say afraid, exactly," I said slowly. "But even *you* must admit there are some horror stories out there. What you see on the screen isn't always what you get in real life, right?"

Chandler studied me so intently for a moment that I was taken aback by his focus. "Sounds like you've been burned a couple times."

That was the understatement of the year, but no way was I about to share.

"You could say that," I added in as nonchalant a tone as I could manage. Inside, I was anything but. I couldn't allow the conversation to continue along that path. Too much pain there. Humiliation. Heartache.

I propped my feet up on the coffee table and locked gazes with him. "So... tell me. What really happened? How did I end up with a photo of your dick on my phone?"

Chandler rolled his eyes. "Oh God. That was totally unplanned. I sent it to a guy I know. I was trying to tempt him away from football, except I got one letter wrong, and sent it to you by mistake."

I chuckled. "Well, it certainly tempted me." I cocked my head to one side. "You seem to have a lot of dates, judging by the snippets of conversation that I've heard."

He snorted. "Dates? Hookups is a more accurate description." His eyes gleamed. "Although a lot of *sex* would be nearer the truth."

"And is that enough for you? Keeping things that casual?" I genuinely wanted to know.

"You take what you can get, right?"

There was an almost wistful edge to his words that revealed much.

In that moment, it hit me. Chandler and I were more alike than I thought. And what followed was a burst of longing that flooded through me. *Could we be* more *than just sex? Would he want that?*

Then I pushed it aside. Such an outcome seemed unlikely, given the way our unorthodox… *relationship* had begun. And it didn't matter how appealing the idea of *more* was. I knew why Chandler had gone along with my proposal. One, he was a slut, and two, he wanted to keep his job.

Except there was this small voice at the back of my mind that said maybe my first assumption wasn't totally correct. There was more to Chandler than I'd previously thought, and this new glimpse sent a shiver of anticipation through me.

It was then that I realized I *wanted* to be wrong.

"Can I ask you something?"

I dropped back into the moment, to find Chandler regarding me with a speculative glance. "You can *ask*, sure," I replied with a slight smile.

"Are you happy with the way this has gone so far?"

Okay, I hadn't expected that.

"Define 'happy'." I knew I was hedging, but I wanted to see where this was going.

"Well, you've gotten your dick sucked, and you've fingered me. Is that how you want it to continue? We proceed to the fucking, and just carry on like that?"

To the point, just like I'd expected, but I was intrigued by the question. "You have some ideas on the subject?"

He didn't reply, but took a drink from his glass. It took me a moment to see the action for what it was—Chandler was nervous.

Okay, this was definitely new territory. Chandler, unsure of himself? He always came across as confident, cocksure, bold even.

I made a decision and shifted closer on the couch, wanting to see how he reacted. There was only a hand's width between us. "What did you have in mind?" I kept my voice low. Then I put down my glass and stroked a single finger along his thigh, starting at the knee and moving higher, stopping just short of the crease in his jeans where the beginnings of an erection were visible.

Whatever he wants to ask, it's a turn-on. My finger's slow journey hadn't fazed him, however.

"Well..." Chandler took another sip. "When you laid out how things were going to go, you didn't mention if we were going to keep it strictly... vanilla." He licked his lower lip, and for one moment, I wanted to be the one tracing the soft flesh with my tongue, before exploring his mouth, pulling gently on that full lip with my teeth, feeling his hands on me...

Whoa. Where did that come from?

I didn't kiss. I *never* kissed. And *I* was the one who touched, stroked, manipulated...

Then the full import of that single word hit home.

"You got something against vanilla?" My words were light, but inside, my heart was pounding. No way. No fucking *way*. I couldn't be that lucky. Of all the guys that had crossed my path, had I finally found one who wasn't about to freak?

Except...

My mind was drawn back to That Question.

I get to fuck you too, right?

What if *Chandler* had ideas about being in control?

Okay. I'm not a control freak. No, really, I'm not. Just because I run a company like clockwork, I say how everything goes, I have a schedule and I stick to it, everyone gets to do what I say, and...

Who was I kidding? Control could be my middle name.

So if we were going to start along that path, I got to say who did what to whom. And it sure wasn't going to be *me* in handcuffs, or tied to the bed, or with a huge fucking dildo rammed all the way up my ass...

"I just wanted to see if there were... options." Chandler met my gaze.

Be still my heart. And for once, I wasn't being sarcastic.

"There might be," I said slowly, retracing that line to his knee, before changing direction and heading back to his groin. Only this time, I molded my hand around his bulge and squeezed hard.

Fuck. His eyes were so huge and so dark.

I didn't loosen my grip as I locked gazes with him. "This what you had in mind?" Then I tightened my grip.

He swallowed, hard. "Fuck, yeah." That

came out as a whisper.

"Just so we're clear? This is how it would be." I smiled. "I like having the upper hand." I loosened my hold on his dick, and he breathed easier.

"Yeah, I sorta guessed that."

I picked up my glass and took a long drink from it. "Seems like we're on the same page." I didn't move back to my previous position.

"Just so we're clear…" Chandler coughed. "I know that was a head rush today when Dean opened the door, but I don't want us getting caught. The whole point about this is that it stays secret. Right?"

"Hey, *you* were the one blowing me while he was talking, remember?" And yes, it *had* been a rush. Part of me had fucking *loved* it. And wanted more. I grinned. "But you have to admit, it got your heart beating faster." Still, he had a point. The complications that could arise if we were discovered didn't bear thinking about. Chandler reported to me, so us fucking had to be some kind of violation of company policy. And if push came to shove, Chandler would be the one to get a warning or worse, and my reputation – and the reputation of my company – would be down the toilet.

It was my company, and I wasn't about to risk it.

Chandler finished his Scotch. "So where do

we go from here?"

"Business as usual. You turn up to work, you do your work, and at the end of the day, you come to my office." I smiled. "Only, this time? I'm going to lock the door."

He laughed. "I was gonna suggest that."

This felt... good, like we'd cleared the air, laid the groundwork... On impulse, I added, "except now that we've talked, I might bring a little extra something in my briefcase."

Chandler reaching down to adjust his hard on was *all* kinds of delicious.

In that moment I wanted to change my mind. I wanted more than a conversation and a drink. But I knew I had to be strong.

I had to be the one in control.

I glanced at the clock. "I think you should go. We've both got work in the morning, and I happen to know your boss is a stickler when it comes to punctuality." I gave him a wide smile.

"Yeah, that boss of mine." Chandler's eyes twinkled as he got up from the couch. "He can be a real hard ass. But you know what?" He headed for the door, and paused, his hand on the latch, his gaze on me. "He has *the* hottest looking ass. And one of these days..."

I got the implication, and chuckled. "Dream on."

Chandler stilled. "That wasn't a 'no no no'. I'm still thinking a definite maybe." That wicked gleam in his eyes was really attractive. "I'm not gonna give up."

"I love a man who sticks to his guns." And I *definitely* wasn't imagining me on all fours, Chandler's hands on my hips, pulling me back roughly onto his thick cock, both of us moaning, both of us close to the edge...

I shoved him out the door and locked it, before either of us said or did something *I* might regret.

3.00 a.m. and I was wide awake. I was in no doubt as to what was preventing me from falling asleep.

Chandler.

He'd revealed a lot, some of it I'm sure unintentionally. I couldn't escape the feeling that beyond the liking for sex, the penchant for spicing things up a little, there was a man who longed for more than that. What shocked me to the core was that *I* wanted more too.

This could get tricky.
This could get... serious.

I didn't *do* serious. I'd started this with one aim in mind–a way to meet my needs, pure and simple. Once I'd realized Chandler was on board with the prospect, I'd envisaged encounter after hot encounter, getting my rocks off, with no fear of complications. I knew where I was with Chandler. He was a known quantity.

Except he wasn't. I'd gotten him all wrong.

That didn't mean I had to let things continue along this particular path. I had options.

I could call it off.

Only, I didn't want to. Why the fuck should I? We were both consenting adults. We knew the score going into this. We were both getting what we wanted, right?

What concerned me more was the way that option made me *feel*. Because I really, *really* didn't want this to end. Had I made a mistake inviting him for a drink? Had I unwittingly taken this to another level? Had he read more into this because of my mistake?

Christ. At this rate, I'd get no sleep whatsoever.

I let it continue, then. But maybe with a few changes. I keep my distance. I remain aloof. I let him see that this evening was just a blip, nothing more.

I could do that. I could be distant. Hell, I could do anything.

I'm the boss.

I liked option two. I could do option two. And some part of my brain clearly liked that option, because I felt the tension draining from my body. Finally. As I drifted off to sleep, one thought

filtered through my head.
All I have to do is not let him in.

Chapter 5

Chandler

"Are you coming, or is it just the way you're sitting?" Dean snickered.

I rolled my eyes. "You need to come up with new material. Just saying." I glanced at the wall clock. Sure enough, it was time for the Friday morning briefing, when we all gathered in the boardroom to get the lowdown on how we'd performed during the week. It was Stu's weekly opportunity to deliver a verbal kick in the ass to those who were slacking, but also to give praise where it was due.

Speaking of Stu…

I hadn't laid eyes on him since that drink at his place. If I hadn't gotten such a positive feeling after Wednesday night, I'd have thought he was avoiding me. He'd appeared to be in a good mood when I left, and *I* certainly was.

So why haven't I seen him?

There was one obvious answer—regret. He regretted asking me for a drink. He regretted our conversation. He regretted stepping over some line he'd drawn for himself, and was slipping back into his more usual position.

So where does that leave me? Our 'arrangement'?

Fucked if I knew.

Then I realized Dean hadn't moved. "Something you wanted?" Except as soon as I uttered the words, I knew what was coming. *Shit.*

"So what happened in your little meeting with Stu on Monday? You were sure you were gonna get canned." Dean smirked. "But here you are. Wanna explain that?"

I heaved an exaggerated sigh. "And I'm damn lucky to be here. I'm holding onto my job by the skin of my teeth."

Dean arched his eyebrows. "Yeah, but how? Because if *I* sent a dick pic to the boss, I'd be out of a job so fast I wouldn't have time to count to ten." He narrowed his gaze. "What makes you so special?" Then he grinned. "Oh, I get it. You're fucking the boss. Sexual favors and all that."

I did another eye roll. "Sure. That's obviously it." I shook my head. "I showed him my texts with Ste, which was pretty embarrassing, I can tell you. Then I explained how it had really been a genuine mistake." My heart pounded.

"And he bought it?"

I glared at him. "Why the fuck *shouldn't* he buy it? That's what happened, right?" Around us, heads turned in my direction, and I lowered my voice. "That's what happened," I repeated.

"Yeah, but bosses aren't known for being reasonable, understanding human beings," Dean commented dryly.

"I got a warning. If anything like this happens again, I'm out on my ear. I'm guessing promotion is gonna be out too." Another sigh. I mentally crossed my fingers, praying he bought it. The last thing I needed was Dean getting wind of this.

Dean cackled. "Then you'd better be on your best behavior. And speaking of which, you'd better get your ass into that boardroom. You don't wanna give him any excuse to fire you."

I got to my feet and grabbed my notepad. "You got *that* right." I followed him out of the office and along the hallway into the boardroom with its large, polished table at the center, surrounded by chairs. Most of the staff were already gathered, chatting quietly. No sign of Stu, but it was still a couple of minutes off ten o'clock.

On the dot, Stu walked into the room and took the vacant chair situated at the end. He gave a polite nod to everyone. "Good morning. Are we all here? Great." He grinned. "Hot enough for ya?"

Laughter echoed around the room. It was shaping up to be a record summer.

"Well, just to let you know, the A/C is working fine." He crossed his fingers. "Famous last words. Okay, let's get down to business." He referred briefly to his notes and started talking, but

I wasn't listening. I was trying not to stare at him.

Could he possibly look more drool-worthy?

He was wearing a dark blue suit that fitted him beautifully. His five o'clock shadow seemed more pronounced than usual, and it gave him a dangerous, sexy look that made me thankful my crotch was out of sight beneath the tabletop. But what *really* got to me?

He didn't look at me once.

He made eye contact with all the other members of staff around the table, but avoided my gaze. Not that he did it obviously, but hell, *I* noticed. I doubted anyone else would.

What came as a complete shock? It hurt.

One week since I'd fucked up and sent him that pic, and something had changed in me. It wasn't that I'd seen his cock up close and personal. It wasn't that he'd had his fingers up my ass.

No. It was that we'd… connected in some way. Nothing earth-shattering, I grant you. But it didn't feel like we were the same two men who'd sat in his office Monday morning, while he coolly put his proposition to me. And I knew why.

I'd begun to think it could be more than mere sexy shenanigans. More fool me. Looked like it was just sex after all.

Did you want *it to be more?*

And now we came down to it. Apparently, I did. And that was the shocker.

Someone nudged me, and I realized with a

shock that the meeting was over. Stu walked out of the room without so much as a glance in my direction.

Fine. At least I knew how the land lay. I got up and filed out of the boardroom with the others, Dean at my side.

"He *really* isn't happy with you, is he?"

So I wasn't the only one who'd noticed. Of course, Dean had knowledge no one else possessed.

"Like I said... here by the skin of my teeth." *And looking more precarious by the second.* I couldn't think about it anymore. It messed with my head. "Okay, I'm gonna get back to work. Those reports won't write themselves." I left Dean at his desk and went over to mine.

That was how I was going to play it from then on. I'd keep my head down and get the work done. That way, I wouldn't have time to think.

I sat down at my desk, and pulled up a file on my monitor. My phone vibrated in my pocket, and I glanced around to make sure no one was looking. Some of my co-workers were real pains in the ass when it came to taking personal calls at work. I slipped my phone out of my pants pocket and peered at the screen.

It was a text. From Stu.

Frowning, I opened it.

Tonight after work. Boardroom. Be there.

Talk about short and sweet. I closed it and put my phone back in my pocket. Despite my misgivings, something coiled and uncoiled deep in my belly.

I wonder what he's got planned? What came immediately to mind was me bent over the gleaming mahogany table, while he plowed into me from behind, stealing my breath with every thrust of that meaty cock.

Okay, so it was just sex. But if it was a choice between hooking up with anonymous guys, getting my rocks off with Ste, or my boss fucking me any chance he got, I'd take Stu Ganford any day.

I waited until the office had emptied, taking as long as possible to collect my things. Fiona nodded politely in my direction as she left her desk, and I returned the nod. That left just me and Stu—and the cleaning staff, whenever they arrived. I picked up my jacket and bag, and headed for the boardroom.

Stu was sitting in his chair, pushed back from the desk, his long legs stretched out in front of him, crossed at the ankles, his hands laced in his lap. His shirt was unbuttoned at the collar, his tie loosened. His jacket hung over the back of the chair.

He smiled as I entered. "Lock the door,

please."

I did as I was told, then stood there, awaiting further instructions. Except I wanted more than that.

I wanted an explanation.

"Have I done something wrong?" I blurted out.

Stu frowned. "Why would you think that?"

"Because one, we haven't spoken since Wednesday night, and two, you wouldn't even look at me this morning."

His brow smoothed out, and he smiled. "I didn't dare. I kept looking at this table, thinking about what I was going to do to you on it." He chuckled. "It was all I could do to keep my mind on my notes. Thoughts of you were a definite distraction. And as for not talking to you...." He arched his eyebrows. "I didn't want to draw attention to us. I didn't think you'd want that either."

I breathed a little easier. "Yeah. That makes sense."

Stu cocked his head to one side. "You weren't happy about the way I behaved." It wasn't a question.

I took a deep breath. "It's just that our conversation ended on a really good note the other night. I couldn't get my head around the change in you, that's all." No way was I about to share my real feelings, and this conversation was veering in that direction. I cleared my throat. "So... what *do* you have in mind for us?"

He smirked. "I take it we're back to business as usual? You haven't changed your mind?"

I snorted. "Only if *you* have."

Stu snickered. "Little chance of that." He bent down and retrieved a bag from the floor. I caught my breath as he removed a very long, *very* thick dildo from it. "Think you can get this in that talented mouth?"

I grinned. "Just you watch me." I dropped my bag and jacket on a nearby chair, walked over to him, and held out my hand.

Stu smiled. "As if it's going to be *that* easy." He slowly licked the base of the suction cup, then stuck it on the wall. "*Now* show me."

Still smiling, I sauntered over to the wall, leaned in, and leisurely took the girthy silicone cock into my mouth. It was a stretch, but I did it.

"Hands flat on the wall. Now speed up."

I did as instructed, making sure to make plenty of noises around it. If he wanted a show, he was going to get one. Then I caught my breath as he moved behind me, slipping his hands around my waist to unfasten my pants. I moaned around the dildo as a cool hand reached into my briefs and encircled my dick, gently pulling on it.

"Oh, someone's eager." Stu's breath was warm on my neck, and for one moment, I wanted to feel his lips there. Just below my ear was a hot spot, one that never failed to turn me on. Except after our two previous encounters, I'd gotten the distinct impression that Stu didn't kiss.

Then all such thoughts fled as he roughly pulled down my pants and briefs to my knees. I caught a *click* and knew instantly what it was. Sure enough, seconds later, slick fingers parted my ass cheeks and rubbed over my hole, before penetrating it.

I groaned around the silicone cock, and pulled off briefly. "Those fat fingers of yours. You couldn't have started with one, you know, and worked up to two?"

In response, he pushed them in deeper. "I think we both know you can take them. In fact, I'm hoping you can take a damn sight more." Before I could question what he meant by that, he pointed to the dildo. "Keep your mind on your job. And I want to see you take it deeper. Impress me."

I resumed fellating the dildo, taking it in as deep as I could, coughing a little when he sawed his fingers in and out of me. When he withdrew them, I groaned again, only to gasp when he pushed in cool plastic slowly and insistently, stretching me wide.

A butt plug? And a fucking big one, judging by the feel of it.

I pulled off the dildo and sucked in a breath. "Foreplay? How thoughtful."

Stu chuckled. "Where do you think the dildo is going next? I thought it only fair to get you ready for it. You did say you wanted me to work up to things." He gave a wry chuckle.

I didn't even flinch. "Not gonna be a problem for me."

Stu leaned in, his breath tickling my ear. "That's because you can't see the big picture." He chuckled again, before gently moving the plug in and out of my ass. "And you've stopped again."

I took the dildo into my mouth once more, doing my best to concentrate on my task while he fucked me with the plug with one hand, and stroked my dick with the other. Finally, after a few minutes, he stopped.

"Okay, stand away from the wall." When I did so, he removed the dildo, before gesturing to my body. "Clothes off. All of them." His white teeth gleamed. "I made sure it'll be warm enough for you."

I hastily toed off my shoes, then undid my tie and shirt. Stu removed his shoes, socks and pants, placing them carefully on his chair. He left his shirt and tie as they were, after freeing all the buttons. When I was naked, my heartbeat racing, he pointed to the table. "Bend over it, legs spread."

I shivered as my chest came into contact with the cool surface. My dick pointed stiffly toward the floor. Stu disappeared from my sight, taking the dildo with him, and apparently the lube too. I shuddered as he eased the plug from my hole.

"Fuck, that's a pretty hole. Especially when you're all open for me. It's crying out to be filled." Stu leaned over, his lips brushing against my ear. "So let's fill it." I moaned as he pushed the dildo into me, taking his time.

"How does it feel?"

"Huge," I gasped out. "But good." God, it did. But what I really wanted was his dick inside me. I groaned when he insistently pushed even more of it into me. "Fuck. How far in is it?"

"I'm impressed. You've taken more than three-quarters of it." Then he began a slow in-and-out motion, fucking me with the silicone cock.

"Your dick isn't going to feel much different," I observed breathlessly. Okay, so it wasn't as thick as the dildo, but it was definitely on the meaty side.

"You think so?" Stu's hand was on my lower back, warmer now, stroking me and squeezing my ass cheek. "You're still not seeing the bigger picture though."

"And what *is* the bigger picture?" I demanded, pushing back onto the dildo, determined to show him I could take whatever he threw at me. I was just warming up.

Stu stilled the dildo inside me. "This." Then I gasped as he slowly rubbed the slick, blunt head of his dick through my crack, pausing at my already filled hole.

He's not going to…

Oh fucking hell, he was. Slowly but surely, Stu pushed into me, until I was fuller than I'd ever been in my life.

"Jesus Christ!" I cried out, unable to move, my fingers scrabbling over the smooth polished surface.

"Fuck, that's a tight squeeze." Stu sounded as breathless as I did.

"Ya think?" I was grateful that he'd paused, stilling inside me as my body adjusted to him. It wasn't my first DP, but it was definitely the most I'd ever been stretched.

He chuckled. "Ready for more?"

"There's more? Because I don't think you can fit anything else in there." Then I groaned as he began to move, sliding his cock languidly in and out, the dildo remaining still. "Oh my God. That feels…"

I had no words. It felt incredible. Yes, I was stretched wider than ever, and I felt every goddamn inch of his cock as he moved inside me, but it was exhilarating. My heartbeat raced, tremors jolted through me, and through it all I couldn't move.

"You have no idea how this looks. If I had both hands free, I'd take a picture so you could see. Your arse, spilt wide, the skin so tight around my dick.…"

"Have I ever mentioned… that I love it when you say arse?"

Stu chuckled. "I think it sounds so much better than ass, don't you?" Then he withdrew both his cock and the dildo, and I had never felt so empty.

"Just me now," he whispered, before filling me with his warm, thick shaft. Only this time, he gripped my shoulders and fucked me, slamming into my ass cheeks, the sound as subtle as a slap.

I couldn't speak. I simply pushed back onto that thick dick, meeting his thrusts, each impact pushing the air from my lungs. Stu didn't falter in his stride, but drove deep into me, his fingers digging into my shoulders, his body slamming into mine.

Lord, the man knew how to fuck.

It wasn't long before we found our rhythm, and fuck, it was amazing. I reached down with one hand to stroke my aching cock, slicking it with pre-cum. When Stu came to a halt, I groaned aloud.

"Want you to ride me," he gritted out, before pulling free of me. He climbed up onto the table and lay on his back, his shirt open, his legs bent, his dick rigid, encased in latex. He held his shaft steady, his gaze focused on me.

Fuck, I wanted to ride that.

I knelt astride him, reaching back to guide him to where I so desperately wanted him, then sank down onto that hard cock. I planted my hands on his chest as I impaled myself again and again, nudging closer to the climax I knew awaited me.

This was going to be an epic cum.

Stu had his hands on my thighs, pushing up with his hips to meet me. "I'm close."

I gazed down at him, his tie still around his neck. I grabbed it, twisting it in my hand until I was pulling his head and shoulders up off the table. Then I rode him like my life depended on it, hips rolling, my body bucking, his dick hitting that spot inside me every single fucking time. Stu nodded, his eyes locked on my face, his lips parted. His hands dug into my waist and his eyes widened, and I knew he was about to shoot.

"Do it. Come inside me," I breathed. I squeezed my body tight around his cock, then did it again and again. Stu cried out, a raw sound that bounced off the walls and ceiling, and I felt that glorious throbbing inside me. I stilled, losing myself in the sensation, my own cock harder than I would've thought possible.

Stu shivered and went limp. I let go of the tie and lowered him to the table, before taking hold of my dick and working the shaft, my body poised for the orgasm that was about to roll over me like a ten-ton truck. When I came, spattering his chest with creamy white, I shuddered, bending lower, wanting to feel his lips on mine.

He reached up and held my face in both hands. "Fuck, you feel amazing." Then he scooped up some of the cum and fed it to me. I sucked on his fingers, relishing every moan that escaped those beautiful lips.

Lips he denied me.

We stayed like that, his dick still inside me, both of us shaking. When at last the tremors died away, Stu eased out of me. "I think we're done. At least, we'd better be, because I don't want the cleaning staff to get wind of this." He grimaced. "I'd better give this room a good spray too. It smells like someone's been fucking in here."

"Yeah, go figure." I'd gotten the message. We were done. I clambered off him and got down from the table, a sticky mess. Stu was right about one thing—the cleaning staff could be there any minute. I pointed to the condom as he removed it from his now limp dick. "Better not put that in the trash."

Stu rolled his eyes. "Gee, why didn't I think of that?" He grabbed a wad of paper tissues from a nearby box and placed the used latex in them, before dropping it into his bag.

I got dressed as quickly as possible, my shirt clinging to the stickiness. Stu got into his pants and fastened his shirt, his head inclined toward the door, obviously listening intently. When we were ready, he unlocked the door, after first checking that he'd picked up the condom wrapper from where he'd dropped it on the floor. The dildo, butt plug and lube were safely stowed in his bag. One last glance around, and then Stu closed the door.

As we reached the outer door of the office, the cleaning staff entered, talking animatedly about their plans for the weekend. I nodded to them, smiling, and Stu greeted them politely. We stepped onto the elevator and the doors closed.

Stu leaned against the mirrored wall. "Wow. Talking about good timing."

I was trying to enjoy that wonderful just-fucked feeling, the delicious ache in my ass, and the endorphins that were busy making me feel like a million bucks. "Maybe for our next session we keep a better eye on the time?" That had been close.

Stu snickered. "What—don't you like living dangerously?" The elevator doors opened, and we got off. The security guard on the main desk nodded to us as we walked along the marble lined hallway to the front door. Beyond the glass, Boston was busy, its sidewalks full of bustling people, their working day over.

Only thing was, I didn't want this day to end.

Stu paused at the door. "That was incredible."

Warmth flooded through me. He didn't have to say that. He'd gotten what he wanted, right? But the fact that he'd bothered to say it meant a lot.

Before I could tell him *I'd* thought it was pretty incredible too, he laid a hand on my shoulder. "Look, I'm going to grab some dinner before I head home. I don't feel like cooking tonight." He hesitated, and I wondered what was coming.

I laughed. "Yeah, I know the feeling. I might do the same." Like I cooked. The idea.

Stu looked me in the eye. "Then how about we have dinner… together?"

Wait—what?

Chapter 6

Stu

I had no clue why I'd said that. And judging by Chandler's stunned expression, he definitely hadn't expected it either.

I didn't take guys to dinner. We met up, we drank until I felt more relaxed, we went somewhere to fuck, and then we parted company. That was it. Full stop. So why the hell was I inviting Chandler?

For the life of me, I didn't know.

Chandler wrinkled his nose. "I was thinking more along the lines of grabbing a shower."

I smiled. "Why? You smell great to me." And there went my mouth again, running off. Then I saw his remark for what it was. "Look, you don't have to," I said quickly. "I didn't stop to think that you might have plans of your own." At least I could give him the out he needed.

Chandler blinked. "Oh. I was about to ask… did you have somewhere specific in mind?"

Okay, that stopped me in my tracks.

"I mean, I'm up for anything," he added.

I couldn't resist. "Tell me something I don't already know." I smirked.

Chandler chuckled. "I'm being serious here."

"So was I." Then it occurred to me—I didn't mind the idea of dinner with Chandler. In fact, it could be a very pleasant experience. "So what are you in the mood for?" It was just dinner, right?

That smile was still in place. "More of what we just had?"

I rolled my eyes. "Food, Chandler. I'm talking food." I had to admit, the easygoing banter felt right. And why not? I'd just fucked him. Sex was a great leveler.

He laughed. "Damn. I was starting to get… peckish again." His eyes glittered. Before I could comment on his appetite, he counted off on his fingers. "I like Italian, Indian, Chinese, Thai—"

"How about sushi?"

Chandler worried his bottom lip with his teeth. It was an adorable look. "I've never eaten sushi. Raw fish, right?"

"Not necessarily." I liked the notion of introducing him to a new food experience. "How about I take you to my favorite sushi restaurant?"

"Like I said. I'm up for anything." He grinned. "I guess I can trust you. It's in your best interests, after all. Can't have me coming down with food poisoning, right?"

I laughed. "I don't see that as a possibility." I gestured to the left. "It's this way. Only about ten minutes' walk from here."

"Good, because I'm starving." He chuckled. "I seem to have worked up an appetite. Go figure."

He wasn't the only one. And having sampled the delights of Chandler's lean body in all its naked glory, food wasn't the only thing I was hungry for.

One appetite at a time.

"I have to be honest." I put down my cup of sake and looked Chandler in the eye. "I don't know what came over me earlier. Asking you to join me for dinner... that's not something I usually do."

Chandler arched his eyebrows. "Should I be flattered?" Then he held up a hand. "You don't have to answer that. Maybe you just didn't feel like eating alone. I know *I* wasn't ready to go home right then."

"You weren't?" Something inside me eased at that.

"And seeing as you're being so honest with me..." Chandler took a sip of sake. "This really is good. I could develop a taste for this. Can you buy it outside of sushi restaurants?"

"Of course you can," I said impatiently. I didn't want to discuss the merits of sake. I wanted to hear Chandler being honest. "What were you about to say?"

He put down his cup. "I don't ask guys to dinner either. So when you asked me…" Chandler shrugged. "What can I say? I liked the idea."

"But you date a lot of guys," I said, perplexed. I'd overheard enough of his and Dean's conversations to know that. Granted, they talked mostly about sex, but there had to be more to it than that. "You don't go out to eat on a date?"

"I told you. Hook-ups, mainly. Put it this way. I don't even get into meaningful conversations, let alone eat."

Then I recalled his wistful expression when he'd said something about taking what he could get. What struck me most was that it could have been me talking. The parallels between his life and mine were uncanny.

So I'd been right. *Chandler might get all the action he wants, but it isn't enough.* A feeling I knew only too well. And just like that, my heart went out to him.

"What happened to you?" I asked quietly. I genuinely wanted to know.

Chandler stilled. "What do you mean?"

Two nights before, I'd been unwilling to share those details. Now? I got the feeling he already knew what I was about to say. Chandler had obviously been burned too.

"Remember the other night? When you said you thought I'd been burned a couple times?" I took a deep breath. "It was just the once, but I swore I'd never let it happen again." I didn't want to even *think* about that bastard. "I get the impression you've been through something similar."

Chandler widened his eyes. "Well, fuck me."

I snickered. "Been there, done that." The humor was welcome relief.

He wasn't smiling, however. "It was bad, wasn't it? Bad enough that you don't trust the strangers you meet."

"Bad enough that I ended up in the Emergency room. Even after that, he wouldn't leave me alone. I suddenly had my own personal stalker. I got a restraining order. From then on, I only dated someone if we had mutual acquaintances. Not that I date guys all that often." Except dating was hardly what I would call it. Yet another thing I seemed to have in common with Chandler.

Maybe that's why I find it easy to be with him. We share common ground.

"Oh my God, Stu." Chandler's eyes were full of compassion. "That's awful. My experiences were a walk in the park compared to that. I'm so sorry you had to go through that." The sincerity in his voice was unmistakable, and it brought a lump to my throat.

I picked up my cup of sake. "How about we

change the subject? No more talk of dating disasters. Let's drink to something more positive."

"What did you have in mind?" Chandler raised his cup.

I didn't hesitate. "To an interesting future."

He was plainly biting back a smile. "That's kind of vague."

I smiled. "It leaves a lot of scope."

The server arrived to ask if we wanted dessert. I nodded and ordered ice cream for both of us. When he walked away, Chandler gave me an inquiring glance. "Apparently I'm having ice cream."

I laughed. "Trust me. You'll love it. Green tea ice cream has a delicate flavor. It's really very pleasant. And it's a typical Japanese dessert."

He drank the last drops of his sake. "This gives you quite a buzz, doesn't it?"

I refilled his cup, sharing the remains of the carafe between us. "There are all kinds of sake. My favorite is one that's best drunk cold. And yes, it also has quite a kick." I gazed at the tabletop, smiling. "I see you liked my choices." Every platter was empty.

He licked his lips. "Enough that I'll be coming back here." Chandler's eyes met mine. "Of course, the company was pretty awesome too. So maybe if I'm to enjoy another meal, I'll need to replicate *all* the elements."

I tilted my head to one side. "Is that your

way of saying I need to be there too?"

Chandler grinned. "Hey, that's a great idea. We should do this again."

Part of me really liked that idea.

The ice cream arrived, and Chandler wrinkled his nose at the color. I snorted. "Have you ever eaten pistachio ice cream?"

"Sure."

"Well, that's green."

He snickered. "Okay. There's green, and there's *Oh My Fucking God That's* Green."

I pointed to his bowl with my spoon. "Try it. You've trusted me so far."

"But it's tea!" He wrinkled his forehead. "I don't even *drink* tea." I gave him a mock glare, and he hurriedly collected some ice cream on his spoon. "Okay, okay, I'm trying it." He tentatively licked the bright green dessert, and his face lit up. "Hey, this is delicious."

I had to laugh. The more time I spent around Chandler, the more I liked him. "See? We all need to try new things."

His eyes gleamed. "Oh really? Well, I've an idea of something new *you* could try."

I had the distinct feeling I knew where he was heading. "Mm-hmm." I narrowed my gaze. "I thought I said something about changing the subject."

"But it's such a *delightful* subject." The hint of a whine in Chandler's voice was comical. "And if you haven't even *tried* it...."

I arched my eyebrows. "I don't recall mentioning that I'd never *tried* bottoming," I said in a low voice. The hitch in his breathing was delicious. I pressed ahead. "But before you get any ideas, I made my feelings very clear, if you remember. I said it would take an exceptional man to get me to bend over for him."

"And if I'm that man?" Chandler said softly. "You'll never know if you don't try."

Not for the first time, I imagined his thick dick spearing into me, allowing me that exquisite feeling of fullness. *And for you, I might.*

Instead of replying, I called for the check. When the server went to find the card reader, Chandler frowned. "Who says you're paying for dinner? Can't I pay my share?"

I waved my hand. "You can get the check next time." I smiled. "Especially as you apparently plan on doing this again." My response seemed to mollify him. I paid the check, and once I'd pocketed my wallet, I got to my feet. Chandler joined me, and we walked slowly out of the restaurant onto the busy street. Traffic hurried past us, and the horizon of tall buildings appeared dark against the backdrop of a reddening evening sky.

"Well, I guess it's goodnight." Chandler put on his jacket and slung his bag over his shoulder.

For the third time in one day, I couldn't put a brake on my mouth. "It doesn't have to be."

He gazed at me with interest. "Really?"

I nodded. "Why don't you come back to my place for a drink?" My pulse quickened. What was it about Chandler that made me want his company? That made me reluctant to walk away from him?

Damned if I knew.

"A drink?" His lips twitched.

I chuckled. "Yes, a drink. Maybe two. Is that acceptable?"

Chandler beamed. "Very."

It seemed I wasn't the only one who didn't want this night to end.

I paid the taxi driver, and then led Chandler toward the apartment building. Neither of us had said much on the way there, but it had been a pleasant, comfortable silence. Now that we got closer to my apartment, however, a trickle of anticipation skittered down my spine. I knew where this evening might lead, and although it had been a few hours since we'd fucked, my dick was already stiffening at the thought of sliding into that tight arse once more.

Better fucking than talking. Fucking was *way* safer.

I opened my front door, and stood aside to let him enter. Chandler removed his jacket and gestured to the living room. "In there?"

"Did you plan on investigating another room?" I asked in amusement, like the idea hadn't already crossed my mind.

"That depends." Chandler paused at the living room door. "Is there a room you'd *like* me to see?"

"Possibly." My heartbeat was racing again.

Chandler smiled. "I thought I came here for a drink."

"Correct." Unable to stop myself, I stepped closer to him and cupped his cheek. "But the drink can wait." I leaned in, my heart pounding, and kissed him on the lips.

Chapter 7

Stu

Chandler stiffened, and I pulled back my hand, my stomach churning. "Something wrong?" I could have sworn he wanted this as much as I did.

He swallowed. "It's just that… I kinda thought you didn't kiss."

Relief bubbled up inside me. "Do you have some strong objections to kissing me?"

His eyes widened. "Fuck no. I've wanted to—"

That was as far as I was letting him go. I pushed him against the wall and sealed my lips to his. Chandler moaned and opened for me, allowing me to explore him. I molded my body to his, conscious of the erection he couldn't hide. I ground my own hard dick against it, loving the way his moans multiplied. He went to put his arms around my neck, but I was having none of that. I grabbed his wrists and pinned them to the wall above his head, before deepening the kiss.

I wanted to fucking *own* that mouth.

Chandler gasped and I drew back. "Whoa." He was breathless as hell. "Slow down."

"Why?"

"Because…" His chest rose and fell rapidly, his

breathing shallow. "Maybe... maybe I want a change of pace."

"*You* want?" I let go of one wrist and dragged his hand down to my steel hard cock, pushing against the zipper of my pants. "Maybe this is about what *I* want."

"I get it, you call the shots, but..." Chandler looked me in the eye, and I stilled. I couldn't help it. There was a nakedness in his gaze that undid me.

"But what?" My voice was softer this time. I wanted to hear what he had to say.

"We just did the whole frantic fuck thing," Chandler said simply. "In fact, every time we've done anything, it's been hard and fast." He drew in a deep breath. "So all I'm saying is... can we try slow and... sensual?" He gave a lopsided grin. "You know, maybe in a bed? Taking our time? I mean, there are no cleaning staff about to discover us. No employees around to walk in on us. What is so goddamn wrong with making it last?"

I was about to tell him that he was right the first time—I called the shots—when something stopped me. His words had conjured up this image of us in my bed, making out, touching, him intimately tracing my body with his tongue...

With a shock, I realized this was something I hadn't experienced in a very long while.

Maybe it was about fucking time.

I took a breath, and there it was, that scent of his that kept stirring me. I locked gazes with him.

"Absolutely nothing wrong with it." I let go of his wrist, took his hand, and led him through the apartment to my bedroom, my heart racing.

Once inside, we resumed kissing, only now it was slow, deliciously slow, and I loved it. We were still standing, we had our clothes on, and I didn't mind. What mattered was the feel of his lips against mine, his hands on my shoulders, his scent in my nostrils. Christ, I wanted to drown in that smell.

Chandler walked me backward toward the bed, and I let him, our mouths fused in kiss after kiss. We both kicked off our shoes, our jackets discarded on the floor. He pushed me onto my back, and I went with it, pulling him on top of me, stifling a moan at the feeling of that hard body against mine. I let him lead, because I already knew the outcome: it would be my cock in his arse, and no amount of sensuous foreplay was going to change that.

But damn, he felt amazing.

Before my brain got too fogged by lust, I emptied my pants pockets, tossing the packet of lube onto the bed, the remnants of my supplies for our after-work assignation. Chandler blinked, and I smiled. "What can I say? I believe in being prepared."

Chandler's eyes twinkled. "Don't tell me. You were a boy scout."

"For two years." I curled my hand around the back of his head. "Now, where were we?"

Little by little, buttons were undone, shirts, belts, pants and socks removed, until all that was left was our underwear. I waited for him to take them off, but he didn't. Instead, he gently pushed me down again, before straddling me, propped up on his arms, bending low to kiss me. I couldn't stop touching him. I stroked his arms, his nape, the back of his head, and all the while he undulated that lean body, his solid dick rubbing against mine, a reminder of where this was leading.

Where we both wanted it to go.

We kissed as he rocked against my cock, both of us feeding the other soft groans of pleasure. I couldn't get enough of his mouth on mine. His kisses were a drug, I was heading for an overdose, and fuck, I just wanted more.

Chandler paused, his eyes glittering in the lamp light. "I wanna taste that cock."

I chuckled. "Don't let me stop you." I caught my breath as he kissed his way down my torso, stopping when he reached my tight briefs. He rubbed my erection through the soft cotton, then pressed his face there, his nose right in against my balls, like he was inhaling me. My already stiff dick was poking above the waistband, and he kissed the head, before going back to nuzzling my balls, burying his nose in the crease between groin and thigh.

"You smell fucking amazing," he whispered. Then he leisurely pulled down my briefs and tucked the fabric under my sac, revealing my heavy shaft and balls. "Oh my God, you are so big."

"It's not like it's the first time you've seen it." I

arched my back as he brushed his chin down the length of my cock. "Fuck, that feels good." The scratch of his almost-there beard on my bare dick was sexy as fuck.

"You like that?" Chandler rubbed his face over my cock, his glasses dislodging in the process. He tossed them onto the bed, and I spread for him. He lay between my thighs, licking my dick from its base to its tip, before taking it deep.

What followed was pure worship as he alternated between licking and sucking, his nose buried in my pubes as he swallowed me to the root. I stroked his head and murmured words of encouragement and delight.

In my entire life, *no one* had ever sucked my dick as good as Chandler. No one even came close.

Except now it was my turn to worship, and I knew exactly where I wanted to start—that delectable arse.

I grabbed hold of his hair where it was long on top, and forced him to look at me. "See that chair over there?" It was a high-backed affair covered in red velvet, with a long, wide seat and arms. "Go and kneel up on it, holding onto the back."

Chandler was off the bed and onto the chair with an eagerness that made me laugh. He knelt on the padded seat, knees as far apart as he could, his arse tilted. He glanced at me over his shoulder. "Come on already."

I let out a wry chuckle. "Someone's impatient. What about taking things slow?"

He rolled his eyes. "What about sliding that huge cock into my ass?"

I laughed as I unhurriedly removed my briefs, my dick springing up and hitting my belly with its usual dull smack. Then I walked over to the chair.

"Just a sec." I pointed to the mirror on the wall. "Turn the back of the chair toward it."

I swear, his pupils enlarged almost instantly. "I like it." He shifted the chair, then climbed back on, resuming his previous position, only this time his gaze was focused on his reflection.

I leaned over, and kissed between his shoulder blades. I laid a trail of kisses down his back, gently stroking the warm skin as I made my way lower, finally arriving at his briefs. His dark crease was visible through the taut white fabric, but I resisted the urge to remove them.

"That is one beautiful arse," I commented, before pulling back the cotton and kissing the cheek beneath. I bit gently, and he groaned. "Just beautiful." I bared more of his firm round flesh, kissing my way toward his crack.

"Stu." My name was a soft whine.

Laughing quietly, I pulled down his briefs to just below the swell of his arse, then spread his cheeks and dove in, licking over his hole. Chandler automatically tilted his arse higher, and I buried my face in his crease, drinking in the rich smell of him, heady as fuck.

"Oh, fuck, yeah, open me up," he moaned. He

dug his fingers into the velvet, arching his back for me.

I couldn't let it be said that I was not an obliging man.

I pulled his cheeks apart and fucked him with my tongue, accompanied by increasingly loud demands to eat his ass. I kept him spread like that while I licked over his pucker in slow passes, loving how he pushed back, eager for more. Loved how his hole loosened for me, getting him ready for my cock that ached to be inside his tight hole…

And my condoms were all the way over in the nightstand drawer.

Fuck it.

I paused, still stretching his hole wide, the pink entrance so inviting. "When was your last test?"

Chandler froze, then peered at me in the mirror. "I'm on PrEP."

"Not what I asked." So was I, but I needed to hear more.

"Last week." He swallowed. "Results are on my phone. You wanna see?"

"Did you get the all-clear?"

"Yes," he fired back. "How about you?"

"Two weeks ago. Same result. I'm on PrEP too." And I badly wanted to be bare inside him.

His eyes were huge. "You want to?"

"Only if you do." Because if he said no, that was just fine.

He said nothing, but stared at me, breathing fast. At last he inhaled deeply. "Then fuck me raw."

I glanced down at my rigid cock, pre-cum already glistening at the slit. I knew there was a lot more where that came from.

"For fuck's sake, get it in me then," Chandler moaned. I stroked his back, then kissed it, moving down his spine to give his hole one more pass with my tongue. Then I couldn't wait any longer.

I smeared the head of my dick and the shaft with pre-cum, before tearing open the packet and squeezing out yet more lubrication. Then I guided my slick cock between his cheeks, his briefs still in place. Slowly, I gave a gentle push, and sighed as his body sucked me in, so fucking tight around my cock. Chandler bowed his head briefly as he accepted the sensual intrusion, until I was all the way inside him.

"Oh yeah," he said with a long, drawn-out sigh. "That feels so good."

I leaned over him, my dick balls deep, and kissed the back of his neck. Chandler shivered, and I did it again, tugging gently on his earlobe with my teeth. Our gazes locked as we stared at the mirror, me not moving inside him. I kissed and sucked his neck as I began to move, just a gentle rocking of my hips. I massaged the back of his neck while I slid in and out of him, soft groans spilling from his lips.

"Fuck, Stu…." More shivers rippled through him, his breath leaving him in short, staccato bursts. I reached around to cup his throat while I sucked harder on his neck, knowing I would leave a mark.

My mark.

When his groans grew louder, I covered his mouth with my hand, and fuck, his eyes widened. He pushed back onto my dick, his moans muffled. I was panting now, aware of blood rushing through my ears, and the combination of my own breathlessness and the noises that poured from Chandler only served to heighten the eroticism.

He reached up to pull my hand away, his gaze focused on my reflection. "Harder," he whispered. "Fuck me."

I nodded, grabbing hold of his shoulders as I rocked faster, sliding in and out of him. Our bodies slammed together, each jolt sending a ripple through his arse cheeks as we connected. The skin on his shoulders whitened where I dug my fingers in, snapping my hips forward with every thrust of my cock into him. Chandler stared at me, his eyes so wide, his lips parted but no words escaping, only harsh breaths.

He gripped the back of the chair with one hand, burying his fingers in the velvet's pile, his free arm jerking as he worked his shaft. His body tightened around my dick, and the sensation propelled me closer to orgasm. Chandler shuddered, and I leaned over to watch the spatter of creamy cum against the deep red velvet, decorating it in a pattern of drops.

I kissed his neck, then whispered in his ear, "My turn." Then it was back to moving inside him, a slow thrust, followed by an even slower withdrawal, gradually picking up speed, the friction deliciously exquisite.

"Come inside me," Chandler gasped out, focused on our bodies moving together in the mirror. He pushed back harder, impaling himself on my shaft, nodding as I panted. I wrapped my arms around his torso and held on, my hips pumping, my dick filling him to the hilt, edging closer and closer.

And there it was, that electricity tingling through my balls and along my dick as I shot hard, groaning as Chandler tightened his body around my cock while it throbbed inside him. I held onto him, the pair of us shuddering, both covered in a sheen of perspiration, the air thick with the smell of sex and sweat.

Gingerly, I eased out of him, loving the sight of him expelling my cum from his body. I had to smile. "I guess it's time to clean this chair." I helped him to stand.

"I can do my bit." Chandler bent over the chair and scooped up some of the cum with his fingers. He held them out to me, and I didn't hesitate. I licked them clean, then sucked on them. Chandler's breathing hitched. "Fuck. Are you *trying* to get me hard again?"

I smiled as I pulled his fingers free. "Why—is there somewhere you need to be tonight?"

He stilled. "What do you mean?"

I pulled him closer, until his chest was pressed against mine. "I mean, tomorrow is Saturday. So… why not stay here? That leaves us all night to get you hard over and over again." I'd uttered the words in a teasing tone to hide what I knew to be true—I didn't want Chandler to leave.

Chandler arched his eyebrows. "And how many times can you come in one night?"

I grinned. "Why don't we find out?"

He bit his lip. "Does the offer to stay the night come with beer? It *is* Friday night, after all."

I had a much better idea. "How does champagne sound?"

Chandler laughed. "You give me champagne, and I may never want to leave," he joked.

I didn't trust myself to speak. I'd just had the best sex ever, and my body was awash with endorphins. Who knew what would come out if I opened my mouth?

Because with one night, something had changed.

Chapter 8

Chandler

I opened my eyes, and for a moment I didn't have a clue where I was. Then I remembered.

Stu's place. Stu's bed.

Stu lay beside me, still sleeping, his hair tousled, his back to me. The sheet was pushed down low, revealing the curve of his ass. An eminently fuckable ass.

I smiled to myself. *Look but don't touch, remember?* That delectable ass was out of bounds. I crept out of bed and headed for his bathroom, aware of the acute need to pee. Once I'd relieved myself, I washed my hands, glancing in the mirror at my surroundings. As bathrooms went, it was pretty ordinary, except for the fact that there was no bath. Instead, glass screened off one end, behind which was a shower, complete with a tiled seat.

Oh baby. What I'd love to do to you in there.

I filled an empty glass with water and drank a couple of mouthfuls. I badly needed to brush my teeth. The last thing in my mouth had been Stu's cum. I opened the cabinet below the sink and spotted several new toothbrushes. I helped myself to one.

Fuck it. I'll buy him a new one to replace it.

Once my breath was minty fresh, I tiptoed back into the bedroom, to where Stu was sitting up in bed, the sheet rumpled around his hips. "Well, good morning."

I lowered my gaze to where the head of his dick was visible above the sheet as he lazily tugged on it. "Looks like it could be a very good morning."

Stu chuckled. "I thought you might like to start your day with some protein."

Somehow I didn't think he was talking about eggs for breakfast.

I climbed onto the foot of the bed and crawled slowly toward him. "Only if you want some too."

His eyes lit up, and he pushed the sheets off him.

I laughed. "I'll take that as a yes."

You know how sometimes you kinda see things in slow motion? Like, you take a moment to stop and really take in what's going on around you? Well, that was my Saturday morning. We lay on our sides, head to tail, enjoying each other, neither of us in any hurry, while sunlight spilled into the room, falling onto white sheets and reflecting on pale walls, the hum of traffic outside easy to ignore.

It was almost... magical, everything moving so leisurely, his hands on my body, my hands on his, and the scent and feel of him filling my senses. And when he reached for the lube without a word, I turned onto my belly, my ass tilted, legs spread wide, awaiting that glorious moment when his cock would slowly spear into me.

What made it heavenly? Stu's arm around me as he languidly rocked into me, his lips on my neck as he kissed me there, before biting gently into my shoulder. His breathing was harsh as he neared orgasm, and by then I was on all fours, impaling myself on that thick dick, squeezing my body around it, milking the cum right out of him.

"Fuck, you feel so good," he whispered as he shuddered through his climax, his cock throbbing inside me, my fingers wrapped around my own dick as I came over the sheet, my body trembling.

But I swear my heart fucking *stuttered* when he gently turned my face toward his and kissed me, his lips soft against mine.

This wasn't fucking. Not even close. Because it felt for all the world like Stu Ganford was making love to me, and fuck, I wanted more.

Stu

By the time midday arrived, I couldn't deny what was going on a moment longer.

Something momentous had occurred.

Maybe it was the unhurried, gloriously sensual sex. Maybe it was the easy way we laughed and joked, talking in bed like we were lovers. Maybe it was the way we couldn't stop touching each other, even once we were clothed. Whatever it was, I knew how I felt.

I didn't want Chandler to leave.

I told myself I was being ridiculous. We'd been fucking for a *week*, for Christ's sake. It was just sex, right? Except I knew I was lying to myself.

Somehow, it had gotten to be way more than sex. But was it like that for Chandler too?

On an impulse, I suggested going out for lunch, and he agreed. I'd intended it to be a bite to eat somewhere local, but when we couldn't decide on a location, I took control.

How we ended up at Joe's American Bar & Grill, with what had to be one of the best views of Boston Harbor, I have no idea. We sat under a blue parasol, the sunlight glinting on the still water, while we ate crispy calamari to die for, followed by grilled chicken salad, and accompanied by a delicious bottle of chilled white wine. It should have been perfect. But if that were the case, why did I have knots in my stomach?

Except I knew, deep down.

It didn't feel like lunch. It was more like a date.

I wiped my lips with my napkin and placed it on the wooden table. "What's happening here?" I said quietly.

Chandler jerked his head up from his plate. "We're having lunch," he said simply.

"That's not what I'm referring to, and you know it." I indicated both of us. "What's happening... here? With us?"

He expelled a breath. "Then it's not just me."

Christ, he felt it too.

I emptied the remnants of the wine bottle into our glasses, then took a drink. "This wasn't what I wanted."

"I know that." Chandler sat so still. "I got the message loud and clear right from the start. But..."

"But?"

He shrugged. "Feels like something's changed." He swallowed. "Look, I knew from the outset this was just sex, okay? And that was fine by me. Fuck knows, I've lusted after you for long enough."

Despite the knots in my stomach, I had to smile. "Oh really? *Now* it all comes out."

Chandler rolled his eyes. "Have you *looked*

in a mirror lately?" He leaned forward, his voice low. "*You* are fucking gorgeous."

"Compliment accepted. And ditto, by the way."

He flushed, settling back into his chair.

"Now tell me what's changed."

Chandler ran his finger down the stem of his wine glass, his gaze focused on it. "I guess... I got to see more of you."

I smirked. "Indeed you did. In my office, on the boardroom table..."

"I'm talking about the stuff I *learned* about you. The insights I got into what makes you tick. I saw Stu Ganford the man, not the boss. I... I saw someone who maybe wanted what *I* wanted."

"And what was that?" My voice had a raw edge to it that I didn't recognize.

"More than a stream of hook-ups. More than just sex. Maybe even..." His gaze flickered upward to meet mine. "A relationship."

My heart was racing. "I see."

Chandler's breathing quickened. "Am I wrong? Have I misread the signs? Because if that's the case, I'll—"

I held up my hand, and he fell silent. I took a deep breath. "It's been a week, Chandler."

His face fell. "I know."

"One week."

"Yeah."

"And the only thing different is we've

fucked."

"Oh yeah?" His eyes blazed. "I came to your apartment. We talked. We had dinner. And last night and this morning didn't feel like fucking."

He had me there. Because I felt the same way.

"So tell me. Am I wrong?" He locked gazes with me.

I seized every ounce of courage and hope I could find. "No, you're not wrong."

He blinked. Blinked again. "Say what?"

I sighed. "Do you know how long it's been since I kissed a guy? Too long. As for having a guy in my bed? Even longer. And yet in the last eighteen hours, I've experienced both those things. With you. That has to mean something, right?" I managed a smile, but inside my heart was pounding.

I was about to open myself up to someone, to lay myself bare, and it was scary as fuck.

"And what if it doesn't work out? What if it all goes tits up? What if—"

I didn't give a fuck about our surroundings. I leaned in swiftly and stopped his questions with a kiss. Chandler froze for all of one second, then melted, a soft noise escaping his lips.

That sound undid me. Because *I* was the cause of it. And damn it, kissing Chandler felt *right*, more right than anything I'd ever experienced.

When I drew back, I sighed again. "Believe me, I'm as scared as you are. I *know* none of this is logical. I *know* it feels fast. And believe me, there's a voice in my read *right this second* screaming, 'what the fuck are you doing?'"

He laughed. "I think that voice has a brother. He's in *my* head." Then his expression grew serious. "So why am I not listening to it?"

I couldn't speak for Chandler, but I knew damn well why I was ignoring it. "I've done the keeping-my-heart-safe thing, and it's lonely as hell. So maybe it's time to ignore logic and go with what my heart is telling me." Words I'd never uttered my entire life.

"And what *is* it telling you?"

I reached across the table and covered his hand with mine. "To take a chance on you. On us." Now that I'd said the words, I knew they were the right ones.

His face softened. "Oh wow. But...can we do that? I mean, working together?"

And that was where it got tricky.

"Stu?"

I released his hand. "There's nothing in the rules that say I can't date an employee." Was there? I had no idea. I didn't get involved in HR. That was Hugh Peters's domain, and I left him to it.

"You sure about that?" Chandler didn't

look convinced.

"No, but I'll take a look." That translated as I'd get Hugh to take a look. Maybe.

"And in the meantime? What happens at work?"

That part was easy. "We do what we did all last week—we don't draw attention to ourselves."

He widened his eyes. "And what about what we were *doing* all last week? Does that continue?"

I grinned. "After work meetings in my office to discuss your... *performance*, Mr. Mitchell? Oh, I don't see why not. Once everyone else has vacated the building, of course."

Chandler shook his head. "We could just meet up at your place or mine, you know. Outside of work. You know, like a normal couple."

A couple. I guess there was no ignoring that fact anymore. We were a couple.

Damn, that felt good.

I raised a finger. "Two points I must take issue with. One, yes we could meet up outside of work, but where would be the fun in that? Didn't you love the thrill of Dean almost catching you with my dick down your throat?"

"I'm not sure 'thrill' is the word I'd use," he murmured. "And what's your second point?"

I grinned. "Since when could either of us be described as normal?" He rolled his eyes. I took hold of his hand again. "But maybe this is where I should mention that I really, *really* like the idea of staying the night at your place, or waking up with you in my bed. So maybe we should carry on, but see each other outside of work too."

"Sounds greedy," he said with a chuckle.

"Like I care." I signaled the server to bring the check.

"Isn't it my turn to pay?" Chandler's eyes sparkled. "Seeing as we're a *couple* and all."

I leaned back in my chair. "Fine. I'm not going to argue."

His satisfied smile made me feel amazing.

As we walked away from the bar, I realized how light I felt. *All this time, all that was missing was a guy in my life.*

Except that wasn't quite accurate.

All that had been missing was Chandler.

I called for an Uber, and we waited by the roadside. "So what are we doing now?" he asked.

I'd already given that some thought. "Is there anything you have to do today?"

"Only shop for groceries, and do my laundry."

"Could you do that tomorrow?"

Chandler narrowed his gaze. "I could. Why? What will I be doing instead?"

I couldn't resist grinning. "Well, I *had* thought about taking you back to my place, tying you down on my bed, and—"

Chandler's hand was across my mouth so

fast, it took my breath away.

"Don't say another word. Just… surprise me." Slowly, he withdrew his hand.

I leaned in and kissed him, taking my time. When I broke the kiss, I looked into his eyes and whispered, "I intend to."

In more ways than one.

K.C. Wells

Chapter 9

Stu

Chandler eyed the cuffs as I fastened them around his wrists. "Are these new, or am I not the first guy you've tied up?" The intake of breath when he saw the straps emerging from the top corners of the bed had been extremely satisfying.

I checked the cuffs weren't too tight, then leaned over and kissed him lightly on the mouth. "I bought these last week. After our conversation where I learned you weren't exactly vanilla."

Yet more proof that he was perfect for me.

"So now what? Tell me what sexual torture you have planned for me." He grinned. "I can't wait."

I glanced at his erect dick, jerking against his belly. "I can't tell," I replied with a smirk. For what I had in mind, I wanted Chandler hard as a fucking rock.

I climbed onto the bed, after dropping the bottle of lube beside him, then knelt between his spread legs. I lifted them into the air, lowering my gaze to his furry crack.

There was my goal.

"Stu?" The note of pleading in his voice halted me. Chandler was staring at me beseechingly. "Let me suck your cock? Please?"

"Now who could refuse such a polite request?" I straddled him, my dick poking down, and guided it to his lips. Sighing, I slowly slid into wet warmth. Chandler did his best to raise his head from the pillow, moving up and down on my shaft. I focused on his lower end, bending over to pull his arse cheeks apart, then dove in, licking over his hole.

Chandler groaned around my dick, before sucking with even more enthusiasm. I let him do most of the work, while I concentrated on worshipping that tight pucker with my tongue. His cock was like a rod of iron, and the noises that poured from his full mouth made me even harder.

He pulled free with a groan. "Come on, surely I'm ready by now."

I sat up and twisted to look down at him. "And there you go again, not seeing the big picture." Before he could respond, I shifted back a little, reached down, and spread my cheeks.

Chandler couldn't fail to get *that* message. I caught my breath at the first touch of his tongue against my hole. "Oh, yes, that's what I want." I rocked my hips, pulling my cheeks apart as wide as they could go, stretching my hole for his tongue. Chandler responded with an eagerness that sent ripples of sensual pleasure through my body, and I ground down, wanting more. His dick jutted into the air, a solid exclamation mark, and I shuddered at what was to come.

White hot need overtook my nerves, and I shifted position, turning myself around to face him. Chandler stared up at me, his lips wet and red.

"For God's sake, Stu," he pleaded. "When are you gonna fuck me?"

I drew in a calming breath. "I'm not." I grabbed the lube, then slicked up his hard-as-fuck cock. Chandler became very still, and I had to smile. "*Now* you're seeing it." I moved back a little, until I could feel his shaft against my hole. I met his incredulous gaze with a smile. "Remember I said it would take an exceptional man to make me bend over for him? Okay, so this isn't me bending over exactly, but the mechanics are the same." I reached behind me, guiding him into position, until the head of his dick was *right there*, ready to penetrate me.

Chandler was holding his breath. For that matter, so was I.

"Looks like I've found my exceptional man," I whispered, before slowly pushing back onto his cock, gasping as the head breached my hole, so fucking wide. I bowed my head, concentrating on the exquisite sensation of being stretched and filled, inch by inch, until finally he was in me up to the hilt, and I had never been so full.

Chandler let out a soft moan. "Fuck, that's tight." He tugged against the restraints. "Stu, please. I wanna touch you."

I wanted that too.

I leaned forward, my fingers fumbling as I unfastened the cuffs. As soon as his hands were free, Chandler placed them on my thighs, gazing up at me with a look of wonder. "Move, baby," he whispered. "As slow as you like. Take your time." I rolled my hips, and he groaned. "Oh my God, that feels…."

Amazing. It felt *amazing*.

I'd never known a sexual encounter to be so hot and yet so tender at the same time. The care he took to move gently, tilting his hips to ease his cock in and out of my body, his gaze focused on my face, was humbling. I placed my hands flat on his chest and rocked back and forth, the burn inside me fading with each stroke of his dick.

Then we both picked up speed, and God, that was even better. I rode him with more abandon, soft cries spilling from me as he grabbed me around the waist to hold me still while he fucked up into me. When the head of his cock connected with my prostate, *fuck*, I knew it. So did he, aiming to hit it as often as possible.

"Close," I cried out.

Chandler was out of me in a heartbeat, pushing me onto my back, only to hook his arms under my knees and slide back into me, slamming into me as we kissed, each thrust punching the air from my lungs. I clung to him as I shot my load between our bodies, crying out at the sheer bliss of feeling his dick throb within me.

"Oh, Stu."

Hearing my name on his lips....

He held me as I shuddered through what had to be the most intense orgasm of my life. He was shaking too, and I wrapped my arms around him, the air filled with our harsh breaths and the smell of sweat and sex.

"You... you are incredible," he murmured, his lips on my neck, my cheek, my forehead, and *finally* where I wanted them, on my mouth.

"Says the man who just fucked the shit out of me," I said with a chuckle when we parted. "If I'd known you could top like *that*, I might not have waited—"

"A week?" Chandler's eyes sparkled. "Does this mean I get to fuck *you* on the boardroom table next time?" I laughed, and he chuckled. "Wow. That feels so weird on my cock."

"And the answer is yes, by the way." A week ago, the idea of him pushing me face down onto that table and plowing into me would have been unthinkable, but now? Heat flushed through me at the prospect.

Chandler's eyes lit up, and he grinned. "Now I can't wait for Monday."

I cupped his cheek. "Hey, don't be in such a

rush. We still have all of Sunday, remember? Unless you really want to go home?" The thought of him leaving made my stomach clench, and that reaction was enough to tell me just how important he was.

Apparently, there'd been a Chandler-sized hole in my life just waiting to be filled.

"How about a change of venue?" he suggested. "Pack a bag, come home with me, and I'll cook us dinner. Then stay the night." That grin hadn't diminished. "We can go to work together Monday morning. Arriving separately, of course. We don't wanna attract attention, right?"

"No, we don't." I liked the idea of continuing, but only when there was no one around.

"You know what's going to be really difficult?" Chandler's voice was soft. "Acting like I don't… feel for you when I'm around you."

I hadn't missed the hesitation, and I couldn't get over the feeling that he'd wanted to say something else. Maybe something way more revealing.

Then all such thoughts were forgotten as Chandler eased out of me, and I sighed at the loss. He kissed me, his lips soft against mine. "Tonight, in my bed. However you want it. I just want you there."

I wanted to be there too.

Then it hit me. *Damn. I let him in after all.*

In more ways than one.
And it felt good.
More than that—it felt *right*.

Chandler

Stu was singing in the shower, and it turned out he could really carry a tune. What made me smile, however, was how goddamn happy I got, just listening to him.

My bed was a rumpled mess, and I knew before the weekend was over, I'd have to change the sheets. I chuckled. My bed had never seen so much action. *And if I have my way, it'll see a whole lot more.*

With Stu.

Lunch down by the bay had scared the shit out of me. Because Stu had nailed it. There was definitely something going on between us, something that had gotten way bigger than after work sex.

A relationship? Jesus fucking Christ, I was in a *relationship*?

The speed of it all was what scared me. I mean, we were talking one week. People just didn't meet someone and have their lives turned upside down in the space of one week, right? There was going come a time when the other shoe would drop, and Stu would realize he'd gotten it all wrong, he didn't want to be with me, he didn't want a relationship...

Christ. It was as if my brain was trying to sabotage the whole fucking deal before it even got off the ground.

My phone buzzed, and I peered at the screen. *Ste.* Now *there* was a coincidence. That was how this had all gotten started in the first place. I left the bedroom and walked into the living room, closing the door behind me. "Hey."

"I know it's late, but I was wondering..."

Yeah, he didn't need to finish that sentence.

"Sorry, Ste. I've got company." And it looked like that particular company was going be around for a long while.

"You gotta be kidding. I've got a severe case of blue balls, and you're already fucking someone? God, my timing is lousy." Ste cackled. "Well, when you're done, do you think you could–?"

"Ste. Things have changed." And wasn't *that* the understatement of the year?

He went quiet for a moment. "You sound... different. You don't sound like you."

"Thing is... I've met someone. And... it's kinda serious." I chuckled. "So serious it scares the crap outta me."

"What–we talking vows here?"

"Whoa, hold on there." I laughed.

"When did all this happen? How come you haven't mentioned this guy before now?"

I sighed. "Because until last week, there was nothing going on."

Ste fell silent.

"I know, it's way too fast, but—"

"Says who?"

Okay, that stopped me in my tracks. "You don't think it is?"

"I don't think there's a time scale when it comes to the heart."

I blinked. "Wow. That sounds almost poetical." And nothing like the guy who came to my place to get his itch scratched on a regular basis.

Ste laughed. "Let me tell you about Simon. He's a guy I work with. He's older than me, maybe in his forties. Well, he met a girl at a party. They dated every night for a week. He couldn't get her out of his mind. At the end of the week, he asked her to move in with him."

I chuckled. "And I thought *I* was a fast worker."

"Yeah, but that was fourteen years ago, and they're still together. See what I mean, Chandler? If it's right…" He paused. "So stop worrying and go with the flow. If it means I've lost my fuck buddy, then okay, I can live with that—if it means you're happy and in love."

My heartbeat raced. "Hey, who mentioned

love? Didn't you hear the part about it only being a week since all this began?"

"You didn't have to mention it. You said it was kinda serious. And what does *that* mean? Hmm?"

"It's too soon," I said quietly, conscious that the sound of running water had stopped.

"Then don't say the words yet. Wait till you can't keep 'em in a second longer. You never know—he might beat you to it."

Noises from the bedroom told me Stu was definitely done with his shower. "Ste, I gotta go."

"Then go. And Chandler?" Another pause. "Good luck."

"Thanks." I disconnected, just as Stu came into the room, a towel wrapped around him, riding low on his hips, his hair damp.

"Everything okay?"

I let go of my anxiety and fear. "Everything's fine. I was gonna pour us a drink."

"Then don't let me stop you." Stu sat on the couch, his legs wide.

I bit my lip. "You gonna stay like that all evening?"

His eyes sparkled. "Actually? I was thinking of ditching the towel." He loosened it, revealing his gorgeous dick that looked like it was raring to go.

I didn't think we were going to make it as far as the bed this time.

Monday
Stu

My phone buzzed, and I knew without looking that it was Chandler. There had been texts flying to and fro between us all day, and I loved it. There had been that one heart-stopping moment when a text arrived just as Fiona was bringing me my coffee, and I'd almost spilled it down my shirt at the sight of Chandler's cock filling the frame. Fiona glanced at me in alarm, and I hastily pocketed the phone, before wiping my mouth with a tissue. When she left the room, I quickly composed a text.

Another dick pic?

Yeah, but this one was intentional.

I had to smile at that. *Where are you?*

His reply was swift. *Restroom. Thinking of you.*

I chuckled. *So I see. I'm flattered.*

Well, I've shown you mine, now you show me yours.

I snorted as I typed. *We've regressed to eight-year-old boys, have we?* Not that I didn't like the idea. I lowered my zipper, and fished out my already stiffening dick. I pumped it for a minute under the desk, my eye on the door in case Fiona returned unexpectedly. When it was hard, I stood, laid it on my desk, and quickly took a photo of it. Then I hurriedly tucked it away, although that was more of a chore.

I intended staying in the office until everything had… subsided.

I sent him the photo, then followed it with a text. *Thinking of you.*

Back pinged his reply. *Thinking of my mouth around it. Or it in my ass.*

Stop. At this rate, I'd get nothing done, and my hard on would be with me all day.

Okay. For now.

So this was going to be the pattern of my days from then on, was it?

I fucking *loved* it.

Chandler appeared at my door. He frowned when he saw me at my desk, a couple of folders in front of me. "Are you still working?"

I put down my pen and gazed frankly at him. "Yes. That *might* be because I didn't get everything done today that I needed to. Care to speculate as to why that might be the case?"

He grinned. "I love it when you go all British. But hey, it's not *all* my fault. You can't pin this all on me." He held up his phone. "I have the proof right here."

I sighed. "Seriously, though, I need to get this done."

Chandler nodded. "Then here's an idea. Why don't I go home and get started on dinner, and when you're done, you join me?" He smiled. "I'll even run you a bath or give you a massage when you get there."

That sounded wonderful.

"You're on. I should only be another hour."

Chandler came into the room, walked around to my side of the desk, and bent down to kiss me on the lips. "I'll be waiting," he murmured. "There'll be dinner in the oven, and me naked on the couch. How does that sound?"

I cupped the back of his head and drew him into a deeper kiss. "Perfect," I whispered against his lips. Then I swatted his butt. "Now get out of here so I can work."

Chandler laughed. "You got it, boss. Just don't stay so late that the cleaning staff are pushing you out of here with their brooms." He left the office, closing the door behind him.

I didn't mind the distractions. I didn't mind that I had to stay late. It was all worth it, knowing there was someone waiting for me to get home.

The door opened, and I grinned. "You can't stay away, can—" I clammed up as Dean Porter entered the room. I frowned. The office had closed half an hour ago, and Fiona had been the last one to leave, apart from Chandler, of course. "Mr. Porter. Is there something I can do for you?"

He smiled. "Yeah, actually, there is. I'm here to discuss my promotion—and my raise, of course."

I blinked. "And what promotion would that be?"

His smile faded. "The one you're going to give me so that I don't tell everyone you're fucking Chandler."

Chapter 10

Stu

Fuck.

I did my best to look affronted. "I beg your pardon?"

He sniffed the air. "Damn, your air freshener is good. Chandler's only just left, and I can't smell a thing in here. No one would ever guess what you've been up to." He waggled his eyebrows. "That's assuming you weren't banging Chandler on the boardroom table."

Okay, that was a little too close for comfort. Either he was a damn good guesser or he had cameras set up. Then I dismissed that idea. Dean wasn't that much of a planner. He was just an asshole.

An opportunistic asshole.

"'What I've been up to?' What, you mean working late?" I gestured to the files in front of me. "And I don't know what delusional, lewd scenario your mind has concocted, but all that's going on here is work, as you can see. Now, please explain yourself, because you're not making any sense."

Dean grinned. "Hey, not that I blame you

for taking advantage. I mean, if one of my employees sent *me* a dick pic, I'd be up for milking the situation for all it's got too."

So he knows about that. Only one way that could happen—Chandler had told him. Worse, he'd *shown* it to him. But why the fuck would he do that?

"The way I see it," Dean continued, "you tried a little coercion to get what you wanted. You've pretty much got Chandler over a barrel, right? I mean, he could be canned for sure. The way I figure it, all those times when Chandler's been late leaving the office—yeah, I *have* noticed—were when you decided to make *demands* on him, shall we say." He glanced at my desk, smirking. "Like that time I came back last week, and you had that coughing fit? Yeah, that all makes sense now." He rotated his tongue inside his cheek, and God, I wanted *so* badly to smack him in the mouth.

"I don't know what you think is happening here," I began, enunciating carefully, "but I fail to see what it has to do with you."

Dean arched his eyebrows. "I'm pretty sure you don't want everyone around here finding out what you've been up to. I'm sure they'd be very interested to learn Chandler is only holding onto his job because you're fucking him. Not exactly the right way to run a business, I'd say. Downright unethical, in fact. So here's what I propose. I get promoted—and no one discovers your dirty little secret. You can screw Chandler on the boardroom table every chance you get." His eyes gleamed. "Sounds like a win-win situation to me."

Right then, I was fervently wishing I was better informed about HR policies. Then it hit me. *What does* Dean *know about HR?* "Supposing everything you've said is true—not that I'm admitting a damn thing—What makes you think anyone would be remotely interested?" I locked gazes with him. "On the other hand, what *you're* doing amounts to blackmail, assuming your suppositions have any basis in fact." Then I reconsidered. It was still blackmail even if his assumptions were a complete fantasy.

Dean cackled. "One. You've got no proof this conversation ever took place, and I'd deny it. Two. I'm pretty damn certain a boss coercing an employee into a sexual relationship would do a hell of a lot of damage to the company's reputation. Now, I'm sure you wanna keep this pleasant, so the way I see it, giving me a promotion is a small price to pay."

God, he looked smug.

"But hey, you don't have to make a decision right this second," Dean said breezily. "I can wait until... tomorrow morning for the good news." He beamed. "I know you'll see my way makes sense. Like I said, win-win for everyone. Have a great night." And with that, he gave me a cheery wave, the bastard, before walking out of the office.

I sagged into my chair. *Now what in the hell do I do?* I tried to clear my mind and look at the situation logically. Dean's attempt at blackmail was tenuous at best. Okay, so I'd crossed a line—for that matter, so had Chandler—but neither of us had done anything *illegal*, for Christ's sake. Dean had definitely crossed a line, and whatever came out of this mess, he wouldn't be continuing with the company, *that* was for certain.

I need to know where I stand. Then I corrected myself. *Where* we *stand.* Because Chandler and I were in this together.

I looked up the contact details for HR, and made a note of Hugh Peters's phone number, hoping he'd be okay to take a call that evening. I wanted this clear in my head before seeing Dean the following day. And that was another thing. He had no proof that Chandler and I were doing anything, except for that dick pic. I needed to know if he'd seen it, because if not, that cast a different light on the whole affair.

For what *I* had in mind I would definitely need proof.

Right then, however, that could wait. Chandler was expecting me for dinner, and we had talking to do. It would be my job to point out this wasn't as bad as it sounded. Except part of me knew what his reaction was going to be.

He is going to freak. And I couldn't blame him in the slightest.

Chandler.

I glanced at the chaos in my kitchen and laughed out loud. I had *never* gone to this much trouble for a guy, and that right there said a lot about Stu. The second I'd gotten home, I'd pulled up the Food Network, checked the refrigerator and cabinets, and set to work whipping up my version of food heaven. Okay, so it was only mac and cheese with bacon bits, but hey, I'd never made it before, and it was a big deal. Because since when did I cook?

Stu had a lot to answer for.

By the time he rang my doorbell, the kitchen was sort of presentable, and the delicious aroma that filled the apartment made my mouth water. I flung open the door and grinned. "I hope you're hungry. Sorry I'm not naked yet, but the clean-up took—" The rest of my sentence died in my throat at his expression.

Now, I know Stu's smiles, okay? There are several different versions. The sexy grin that gets my heart fluttering, the polite smile he gives during his meetings when someone's had a stupidity spasm and he's trying not to react... And what I was seeing right then was *the* most fake smile ever.

Something was wrong.

"Can I come in?"

That was all it took for my heart to start pounding. "Well, of *course* you can come in. You're having dinner with me, remember?"

The way he looked made me think that wasn't a certainty.

I stood aside and let him enter. "Stu? What's wrong?" The mac and cheese was in the oven and it wasn't about to burn. We had time to talk.

He walked into the living room. "What have you got to drink around here?"

I gestured to the shelf next to the TV. "Vodka, whiskey, Baileys... hell, I think I still have half a bottle of Midori." I fell silent as he walked over and poured himself a measure of whiskey. "Am I gonna need one of those too?"

Stu paused, then reached for another glass.

Is he breaking up with me? Fuck, we've only just gotten together. Something about his quiet manner made my scalp crawl. "Stu, you're worrying me."

He came over and held out a glass. "The important thing to remember here is that it's not as bad as it sounds."

I swallowed, then took a quick swig of whiskey. "Okay, now you really *are* worrying me. *What's* not as bad as it sounds?"

Stu gazed at me. "Did you show that dick pic to anyone?"

I bit my lip. "Now, which dick pic are we referring to? Because there have been a couple." Then I got it. "You mean, the one I sent you by accident?" He nodded. "Nope, no one."

"But you did tell Dean Porter about it."

Ice crawled over the skin on my arms. "Yeah, I did. The night I sent it."

"Why, for God's sake?"

I stared at him. "He called me right after I got your email demanding to see me. And just then I was a mess."

"But he's not seen it."

That ice was spreading, reaching through my skin, through flesh, into my heart. "Stu, what's happened?"

He took a long drink from his glass. "What's happened is your buddy Dean is trying his hand at a little blackmail. He doesn't have any actual *proof* that we're fucking, but he's made some pretty good guesses. But now I know he's not seen that pic, I can make my move."

"What does he want?" Fuck Dean. Fuck him all to hell.

"A promotion. Or else." Stu closed the space between us and cupped the back of my neck. "Now listen. You're not to worry about this."

I gaped. "Not worry—if he doesn't get what he wants, *then* what? He blabs, I lose my job, God only knows what will happen to your company's reputation, and—"

Stu drew me closer. "Listen," he said firmly. "I am going to look into this. We haven't done anything wrong. I'm going to talk to HR and find out where we stand, okay? But you are *not* going to lose your job. Why in the hell should you? If anything, you'll be the victim in their eyes. You know, the big bad boss coercing you into sex..."

"But what if HR says we shouldn't be—"

Stu stopped my words with a kiss, and for a moment, my fears bled away. When we parted, he looked me in the eye. "This is *not* going to put an end to us, you got that?"

"You can't promise that though, can you?" I felt sick to my stomach.

The hesitation before he spoke filled me with dread. "No, I can't make promises right this second. There's someone I have to talk to first. But I am not going to let that... bastard spoil the best thing that has ever happened to me, okay?" He stroked my cheek. "And that would be you, Chandler Mitchell. In just over a week, you have turned my life upside down, and I am not about to lose you." He sniffed up. "Dinner smells amazing, but to be honest—"

"You've lost your appetite." So had I.

Stu nodded. "Would you mind if I went home? There's some stuff I need to do, and ...."

I attempted a smile. "I don't think I'd be

much company anyhow this evening." I wanted him there, but I wasn't going to make demands. He had enough to think about.

Stu leaned in and kissed me again. "Please, don't worry."

"Yeah right. You've got about two hopes of that happening, and Bob died ages ago."

He chuckled. "Where did you dig that one up?"

"Something my dad used to say." I locked gazes with him. "Go home. I'll see you in the morning at work."

He brushed his fingertips over my cheek. "I'll miss you tonight."

"Ditto. Now go. You have stuff to do." I cocked my head to one side. "Is it stuff that might help us?"

"Possibly. I don't know for sure. Call it research." Stu gave me another kiss. "Can the food be saved for tomorrow night?"

I nodded. "Let's hope by then I'll feel like eating."

"Let's hope by then we're both feeling like it." Stu put down his glass and headed for the door. I followed him, watching as he walked toward the stairs. When he was out of sight, I closed the door and bolted it.

I am gonna fucking kill *Dean.*

I walked into the office, my heart quaking. I'd gotten about two hours' sleep, and I hadn't felt this rough in a while. When the sun came up, I came to a decision, one that made me even sicker than the previous night. I knew Stu would pull out all the stops to fix this—I just doubted HR would let him do it.

That left it up to me. Because there was something *I* could do that would make it all go away.

Hardly anyone else had arrived, but there were still thirty minutes to go until the start of the work day. I figured I'd catch Stu while it was quiet. However, when I got to Fiona's desk, Stu's door was closed and Fiona was peering intently at her monitor. She glanced up with a frown as I approached. "I'm sorry, but Mr. Ganford can't see you right now. He's in a meeting."

"That's okay. I just wanted to leave this for him." I placed a long white envelope on the corner of her desk. "Will you make sure he gets it?"

She smiled. "Of course." Then she went back to work.

I returned to my desk, my feet like lead. *Well, too late now. Unless you wanna go and get it back.* Except I wasn't about to do that. This was the only solution, and I knew it.

As I pulled out my chair to sit, I spied Dean en route to the restroom. Just the sight of his self-satisfied grin made my blood boil. I followed him in there.

Dean glanced over his shoulder as he stood at the urinal. "Morning." Then he finished peeing and flushed.

"Morning?" I glared at him as he crossed the tiled floor to the sink. "That's all you have to say for yourself?"

He blinked, then nodded knowingly. "Ah. So he told you. When was that? In bed last night?" That smile was so fucking *smug*, and I longed to wipe it off his face. Preferably with my fist.

He finished drying his hands, then stood there, smirking. "Well, are you gonna let me get past you so I can go to my desk? We can't *all* be the boss's little pet. *Some* of us have to work for a living."

"You're not going anywhere until I've had my say." I was doing my best to keep a hold on my temper, but damn, it was hard.

"Sorry," Dean said with a grin. "Not interested." He tried to push past me, and I saw red. I shoved him back, sending him tumbling to the floor, his jaw connecting with the sink on the way down.

Dean glared at me from the floor. "What the fuck?" He rubbed his jaw. "Where do you get off shoving me like that? What's your problem?"

I gaped. "Are you fucking for *real*? You just tried to blackmail the boss."

Dean got to his feet, still holding his jaw and wincing. "Look, we all know you're not gonna lose out here. He's not gonna jeopardize his company. I'll get what I want, and he'll get what he wants, which I presume is your ass on tap. Everybody's happy."

I curled my hand into a fist and he flinched. I guess he thought I was going to hit him. I took a deep breath. "You know *fuck all* about what's really going on here." Not trusting myself to say another word, I stormed out of there, heading for the main door. I was *so* done.

The best place I could be right then was home, where I could start looking for another job.

Stu

I shook Hugh Peters's hand. "Thanks again for coming in early. And again, my apologies for calling you at home last night. I promise I won't make a habit of it."

Hugh smiled. "No problem. And I'm glad we were able to sort things out."

I chuckled. "Well, I know a lot more about HR than I did this time yesterday, that's for sure." Seeing as I'd spent the evening reading all the policies...

Shame flushed through me. It was my company, for Christ's sake. I should have made it my business to know about everything, not just leave it to others.

Hugh cleared his throat. "Glad to hear it. I'll write up this meeting and email a copy to you. I'll CC Chandler too, once he's paid me a visit." He gave me a speculative glance. "He'll be in to see me today, right?"

"Of course." I'd tell Chandler as soon as Hugh had gone. "Thank you." I walked with him to the door, and as he spoke with Fiona, I noticed Dean in the background. *Of course he's early today.* I went to my desk and got things ready. I knew it wouldn't be long.

Chandler could wait. I had Dean to deal with first.

Sure enough, barely five minutes elapsed before my phone buzzed. "Mr. Ganford? Dean Porter to see you."

"Send him right in."

Dean still wore that same self-satisfied expression. He didn't sit, but stood in front of my desk. I gave him a cursory glance, noting the darkened skin on his jaw. "Are you all right?" I gestured to his face.

"It's nothing. I fell." He stared at me. "So… do we have an understanding?"

I laced my hands together on my desk. "There's still something that requires clarification."

"And what would that be?"

"Well, you've asked for a promotion in return for your silence, correct?"

"Correct. But don't forget I want a raise too."

"How do I know that would be the end of it? What's to stop you from demanding another wage increase? Another promotion?"

"You're just gonna have to trust me on that." Dean grinned. "Look, you're getting what you want, right? I'll keep my mouth shut about you and Chandler as long as my career here stays on an even keel. I'm not a greedy man. Just make sure when the annual bonuses are announced that my name is on the list, and we'll be sweet."

Thank God Dean was not the sharpest knife in the drawer.

I leaned back, stretching out my legs under the desk. "Have you ever read this company's HR policy, Mr. Porter?"

"Nope." He looked like he couldn't have cared less.

"Well, you should have, before you made your demands. Particularly the section on relationships between staff." A section I was now thoroughly aware of.

Dean snorted. "Relationships? Isn't that a bit grand for describing your arrangement?"

"On the contrary. It describes the situation perfectly. So when I met this morning with Hugh Peters from HR, to disclose the fact that Chandler Mitchell and I are in a relationship, he made note of it."

"You're... you're dating him?"

I opened my eyes wide. "Why, yes. Of course, if you'd read the policy, you'd know it's not against company rules for a boss to date an employee. Consensual relationships do occur in the workplace, after all. Where it becomes a little... trickier is when you have a romantic or sexual relationship between coworkers where one individual has influence or control over the other's conditions of employment. We can't have concerns being raised about favoritism, bias, ethics, or conflicts of interest, can we?"

"Exactly! You're his boss."

I nodded. "Which is why I disclosed the relationship. I then gave Hugh assurances that Chandler's line manager would no longer be myself, but Bev Tyndale. All that's required now is for Chandler to make *his* disclosures, and everything is then above board, out in the open."

Dean's face fell. "I see."

I leaned forward, hands back on the desk. "Which takes away your ability to blackmail me, doesn't it? It does, however, leave us with another issue, that of your continued employment within this company."

Dean paled. "But... you just said it... I can't blackmail you if I've got nothing to hold over you."

"But you did attempt blackmail, Mr. Porter, and I'm not going to stand for that." I picked up my phone that was lying on my desk beneath a sheet of paper. "And here is my proof. I've been recording this conversation." I stopped the recording and placed the phone in my drawer.

"That's illegal," Dean ground out.

I wagged one finger. "A conversation can be recorded as long as one party is aware. That would be me." I picked up the handset. "Fiona, would you call Security and have them come to my office, please? ...Yes, immediately... They're to escort Mr. Porter to HR where he'll turn in his badge and keys, plus any company property he has in his possession.... Then could you...? Oh, thank you." I replaced the handset, then gave Dean my full attention. "Security will watch you clear your desk, then they'll escort you from the building. Fiona will have your letter of dismissal typed up and ready for you by the time you leave."

Dean remained silent, his face tight.

The knock at the door came faster than I'd anticipated. Two security guards entered, and politely asked Dean to accompany them. I thanked them, not giving Dean a second glance. Once they'd gone, I got on the phone to Hugh and apprised him of the situation. Only then did I expel a long, shuddering breath.

Thank God that's over.

My hand trembled as I picked up the handset again. "Fiona, could you ask Chandler Mitchell to come by my office?" No more text messages. Nothing to invite suspicion or speculation. I was *not* going to lose him.

"Yes, sir."

A minute or two later, there was a knock at my door, and I smiled. Fiona stuck her head around it. "Chandler's not here. Morgan says he left a while ago." She held out an envelope. "He asked me to make sure you got this."

I took it, puzzled. "Thank you." When she closed the door, I opened the envelope. My stomach clenched when I read that ominous first line. *Oh Chandler.* I got up and put on my jacket, before slipping the folded sheet into my inside pocket. Then I grabbed my phone and my briefcase, and left the room.

"I have to go out," I told Fiona. "Cancel all meetings for the rest of the morning." Hopefully I'd be back by lunchtime, if I could sort out this mess.

I *had* to sort it out.

Chandler

I glanced at the bottles of alcohol on the shelf, before dismissing the idea. Coffee was a much better option. I figured Stu had to have read my letter by now. My phone was silent, however. Not a good sign.

The doorbell rang, and I gave a start. *Who in the hell can that be?* I opened the door and froze when I saw Stu standing there, my letter in his hand.

"What… what are you doing here? You're supposed to be at work."

Stu raised his eyebrows. "So are you. And I'm here to give you back your letter." He gave me a pointed stare. "Do I get to come in?" I stood aside, and he strode into the apartment. I'd barely closed the door when he sighed heavily. "Why would you resign?"

"Because it solves everything," I explained. "Dean has nothing to blackmail you over if I'm not there."

"Dean has nothing to blackmail me over anyhow. And if you'd *trusted* me, I could have told you all that this morning, as soon as my meeting with Hugh Peters was over."

I frowned. "Hugh Peters from HR?"

He nodded. "By the way, now I've told him we're in a relationship, you have to tell him too." His eyes sparkled. "Just so he knows I told him the truth, and I'm not abusing my position of power."

I caught my breath. "You told him? But... aren't there rules about—"

"Bosses screwing their subordinates?" Stu grinned. "Except I'm no longer your line manager. That is now Bev. And she'll know about us too. Everyone will."

Okay, that stopped me in my tracks. "Oh fuck. Dean will hate that." Heat flushed through me. "By the way... I sort of... shoved him in the restroom. He went flying. After his jaw connected with a sink."

"Dean?" Stu frowned for a moment, then his eyes widened. "That was you? Nice one. And don't worry about Dean. He won't be there. I fired him."

"You—" My jaw dropped. "When?"

"Right before Fiona gave me your letter of resignation. See what happens when you sneak out of work? You miss all the fun. And speaking of work..." He slowly tore the letter in two. "That never happened."

Relief flooded through me. "Okay. We back to business as usual?"

Stu nodded. "Except there will be no more sexting during office hours, you got that?"

I'd got back some of my usual sass. "What about kissing? Is that allowed? And what about fucking on your desk?"

Stu chuckled. "And *there's* the Chandler I know and love." Then he stilled. "Which wasn't meant to be a flippant statement, by the way."

So many emotions were in play inside me right then: elation, excitement, hopefulness… "I have this fluttering in my stomach," I whispered.

"Me too." Stu moved closer.

"My pulse is racing."

"Mine too." Closer still.

"My knees feel weak."

"My heart is hammering," Stu confessed. His hand was so gentle on my face. "I wonder what it all means."

Deep down, I knew, but it still felt too soon to let the words out. Then my heart stuttered when he brushed his lips against mine, the kiss deepening as he took me in his arms.

"Chandler," he whispered.

"Yes."

"Lovely though this is…" He grinned. "I have a company to run. You have a job to do. And I don't want everyone thinking we took the morning off to make love."

I smiled. "Now that's a lovely thought." Then I shivered when he kissed my neck. "S-stop that. You know what it does to me."

Stu drew back. "You're right. This can wait until tonight, when I finally get that dinner you promised me, and you naked on the couch."

That thought would keep me going all day.

"But later…" Stu kissed me on the lips, his hands gently cupping my head. When he broke the kiss and pulled back a little, his gaze met mine, and I shivered at the intensity of it. "I promise not to be flippant."

My heart…

I led him to the front door. "I think I'm going to enjoy my new status. Even if it doesn't come with any benefits."

He frowned. "What new status?"

I beamed. "The boss's boyfriend."

That made him smile too. "Get used to it, sweetheart. You're going to be the boss's boyfriend for a very, very long time."

I could live with that.

As I locked the front door, I had to laugh.

"What's tickled you?" Stu asked.

I leaned in and whispered, "I've just realized I won't find it difficult to get laid on a Friday night ever again." If I had my way.

Stu smiled. "Friday night? *Every* night." His eyes gleamed mischievously. "And maybe lunchtimes too, if I lock the office door."

"In that case, I think we need to invest in a new piece of office equipment."

He arched his eyebrows. "What, precisely, do we need?"

I chuckled. "A gag." Then I reconsidered. "Actually, we'd better buy two to be on the safe side." Along with a few other bits that might prove useful.

I wonder how he'd feel about being tied to

his chair while I fuck him?

Work was looking more interesting by the second.

Epilogue

Three months later
Chandler

"And we're done." Bev smiled as she added her signature to the Performance Review form. She leaned back in her chair. "Everyone is talking about you."

I blinked. "What have I done now?" I'd gotten used to the comments once it became common knowledge that Stu and I were dating. Some coworkers had even tried to take advantage of the situation, but word soon got around–we were playing this by the rules. No favoritism. No unexpected promotions. Once they'd realized there was nothing to be gained from sucking up to me, things went back to normal.

Thank God.

"What have you done?" Bev's eyes sparkled. "You've transformed the boss."

I snorted. "Yeah right."

"No, seriously. He laughs more now than he ever did. He jokes around, he smiles more… You've even managed to remove that stick from up his ass."

"Oh, come on," I remonstrated. "He was

never *that* bad. He was just a bit… British, that's all."

"Then maybe you're rubbing off on him." Bev bit her lip. "Metaphorically speaking."

I was glad I'd finished my coffee by that point.

"Okay, let's set a date for our next meeting." Bev scrolled on her tablet, and I got out my phone to go to Calendar. As I did so, it vibrated in my hand, and I saw a text from Stu. Not thinking, I clicked on it–and promptly erupted into a coughing fit.

"Are you okay?" Bev asked anxiously.

"I'm fine," I croaked, fighting for breath, unable to take my eyes off the screen.

It was a photo of Stu's dick, filling the frame. But what got my attention was the cock ring nestled snugly around the base.

Talk about fighting dirty. And speaking of dirty, I knew exactly what I wanted to do with that solid shaft.

"Something important?" Bev's voice pulled back.

I coughed again, and swiped it out of sight. "It can wait." Yeah, it could wait until I got my hands on him. This was *not* playing by the rules.

We agreed on a date, and I made a note of it. I thanked Bev, then left her office, on a mission. Fiona arched her eyebrows as I approached her desk.

"Is it lunchtime already?"

I gave her a polite smile. "Almost. Is he busy?" Stu and I usually spent the lunch hour together in his office, eating and talking. And occasionally giving and receiving blow jobs when the need was great.

Who was I kidding? The need was always great, especially on days that ended in a y.

At least he'd gotten into the habit of locking the door.

Fiona grinned. "Do I buzz you in, or do you want to surprise him?"

"Oh, I think he's expecting me." I walked past her desk and pushed open the door to Stu's office.

He was sitting behind the desk as usual, grinning. "Fancy seeing you here."

I closed the door behind me. "No sexting during office hours, you said. Remember? And we've managed to stick to that since we announced we were an item. So why now?"

Stu's eyes glittered. "Well, I had to get your attention somehow, and this seemed the best way." He picked up his handset. "No more calls until after lunch, thanks, Fiona." Then he replaced it.

I widened my eyes. "See? You do know how to use a phone after all. You could have called me." I sighed. "Okay, you got me here. What's so urgent?" I folded my arms. "Don't tell me you're in dire need of a blow job. You had one, not four hours ago before everyone else arrived."

Stu pushed back his chair, and I gasped. "Why is your dick out?" His pants and briefs were pushed down to his knees. His shaft was standing to attention, the cock ring no longer there, but something was tied around its base—a red ribbon.

Stu held a finger against his lips. "Quiet. Do you want Fiona to hear you?"

I chuckled. "I don't think she'd be in the least bit surprised." I walked around his desk to get a closer look. "Stu... why is there a key hanging from your cock?"

"Take it off then." His voice held a tremor that I usually associated with those times when we were in bed. When he was balls deep inside me, looking at me like I hung the moon.

Precious times.

I knelt beside his chair, then carefully untied the ribbon, his dick jerking as I removed it. I stood quickly, the key in my hand. "This is the key to your apartment."

"Yes," he said simply.

"But I already have your spare key."

Stu's eyes were warm. "Call it... symbolic."

Okay, he'd lost me. "I don't get it."

Stu rolled his eyes. "I'm giving you a permanent key to my apartment. Because I want it to be *your* apartment too."

Light dawned. "You... you want me to move in with you?"

He beamed. "*Now* you're getting it." Then his smile faltered. "Unless you think it's too soon?"

No way was I gonna let him worry about that.

I knelt again. "I think it's time I shared something I've been meaning to say for a while now."

"Okay," he said slowly.

I reached out and cupped his cheek. "Love you." It wasn't like I hadn't known that the day he fired Dean. But he hadn't said it yet, and I figured one of us needed to take that step. I was fine with it being me.

Stu expelled a long breath before taking my face in his hands. "Love you too." Then he pulled me closer into one of those kisses that always sent my heart soaring. The ones that *always* said more than words.

"That wasn't as scary as I thought it would be," Stu murmured against my lips.
I pulled back, staring at him incredulously, and he chuckled at my obvious surprise. "Of course I was scared. I've never said those words in my life."

"Me neither." I couldn't help it. I kissed him like my life depended on it, and he gave as good as he got. I felt so fucking *light*.

"Chandler," Stu murmured again.

"Hmm?" I didn't want to stop kissing him.

"You forgot something."

I pulled back with a frown. "What?"

Stu grinned. "You didn't lock the door. You're slipping."

"Well, *you're* the one sitting there with your dick hanging out. You could've reminded me."

Stu chuckled. "I was busy. Someone just told me he loves me. I got distracted."

"*You* were distracted? What about sending me that photo? When I was in the middle of a performance review with Bev? What do you have to say for yourself, *Boss*?"

Stu blinked. "Oops?"

I shook my head, laughing. "Do you have any idea what you're taking on? I mean, you've seen my place. Minimalist is not in my vocabulary."

Stu shrugged. "If you mess it up too much, I have a flogger and I know how to use it."

I caught my breath. "Damn. You always know the right thing to say, don't you?" I glanced around.

"What are you looking for?"

"That cock ring. What did you do with it?"

Stu smiled. "It's back in my bag. Why?"

"I was just thinking of borrowing it."

It was Stu's turn to catch his breath. "Tonight?"

I nodded. "Tonight." Then I glanced at his rigid dick. "But in the meantime… it seems a shame to let this go to waste."

Stu's eyes sparkled. "Lock the door."

I chuckled. "You're the boss."

The End

About the author

K.C. Wells lives on an island off the south coast of the UK, surrounded by natural beauty. She writes about men who love men, and can't even contemplate a life that doesn't include writing.

The rainbow rose tattoo on her back with the words 'Love is Love' and 'Love Wins' is her way of hoisting a flag. She plans to be writing about men in love - be it sweet and slow, hot or kinky - for a long while to come.

Coming Soon…

The third – and final – instalment of Merrychurch Mysteries – A Novel Murder.

Jonathon de Mountford is struggling to placate his father and keep his boyfriend, Mike Tattersall, happy, but it's proving difficult. Offering to host the first Merrychurch Literary Festival proves to be a welcome distraction. But the small event takes on new proportions when famous author Teresa Malvain agrees to appear. She's a former resident of Merrychurch, coming home after seven years to talk about the inspiration for her murder-mystery series, set in a quaint English village.

Life imitates art when she dies suddenly, apparently the result of a severe allergy. Then it becomes apparent that Teresa was not universally liked. When Jonathon and Mike take a closer look at Teresa's stories, they realize her fictional village isn't so fictional after all. If they're right, there are a few people out there who don't want anyone else reaching the same conclusion. Has someone in Merrychurch already gotten away with murder?

Jonathon and Mike can't resist investigating her death, aided by a couple of people keen to help them discover the truth. But they're trying to work out what is fact and what is fiction, and the line between the two is constantly blurring. And as for their relationship, Jonathon finally comes to a decision....

Book #1 – Truth Will Out
Book #2 – Roots of Evil

Available titles

<u>Learning to Love</u>
Michael & Sean
Evan & Daniel
Josh & Chris
Final Exam

<u>Sensual Bonds</u>
A Bond of Three
Le lien des Trois
A Bond of Truth

<u>Merrychurch Mysteries</u>
Truth Will Out
Au nom de la vérité
Roots of Evil

<u>Love, Unexpected</u>
Debt
Dette
Il Debito
Schuld
Burden

<u>Dreamspun Desires</u>
The Senator's Secret
Le secret du Senateur
Der Verlobte des Senators

Out of the Shadows
Als die Einsamkeit wich
My Fair Brady
Under the Covers

Love Lessons Learned
First
Zum Ersten Mal Liebe
Prime Volte
Waiting for You
Step by Step
Pas à Pas
Schritt für Schritt
Un passo alla volta
Bromantically Yours
BFF
BFF Best Friends Forever (Italian Version)
Gerstern, Jetzt und Auf Ewig

<u>Collars & Cuffs</u>
An Unlocked Heart
Trusting Thomas
Someone to Keep Me (K.C. Wells & Parker Williams)
A Dance with Domination
Damian's Discipline (K.C. Wells & Parker Williams)
Make Me Soar
Dom of Ages (K.C. Wells & Parker Williams)
Endings and Beginnings (K.C. Wells & Parker

Williams)

Un Coeur Déverrouillé
Croire en Thomas
Te Protéger
Valse Hesitation

Herz Ohne Fesseln
Vertauen in Thomas

Secrets – with Parker Williams
Before You Break
An Unlocked Mind
Threepeat
On the Same Page

Avant que tu te brises
Un Esprit Libéré

Personal
Making it Personal
Personal Changes
More than Personal
Personal Secrets
Strictly Personal
Personal Challenges

Une Affaire Personnelle
Changements Personnels

Plus Personnel
Secrets Personnels
Strictement Personnel
Défis Personnels

Una Questione Personale
Cambiamenti Personali
Piú che personale
Segreti Personali
Strettamente personale
Sfide personali

Persönliche Entscheidungen
Persönliche Veränderungen
Mehr als Persönliche
Persönliche Geheimnisse
Streng Persönlich
Persönliche Herausforderungen

Confetti, Cake & Confessions
Confetti, Coriandoli e Confessioni

Connections
Connexion

Saving Jason
Per Salvare Jason
Jasons Befreiung
A Christmas Promise
The Law of Miracles

My Christmas Spirit

<u>Island Tales</u>
Waiting for a Prince
September's Tide
Submitting to the Darkness

Le Maree di Settembre
In Attesa di un Principe
Piegarsi alle tenebre

<u>Lightning Tales</u>
Teach Me
Trust Me
See Me
Love Me

<u>Unverhoffte Liebesgeschichten</u>
Lehre Mich
Vertrau Mir
Sieh Mich
Liebe Mich

Il Professore
Fidati di me

<u>A Material World</u>
Lace
Satin

Silk
Denim

Spitze
Satin
Seide
Jeans

Pizzo
Satin
Seta
Denim

<u>Southern Boys</u>
Truth & Betrayal
Pride & Protection

Kel's Keeper
Kels Hüter

Here For You

Double or Nothing
Back from the Edge
Switching it up
Scambio di ruoli
Out for You
State of Mind

Anthologies

Fifty Gays of Shade
Winning Will's Heart

Come, Play
Watch and Learn

Writing as Tantalus
Damon & Pete: Playing with Fire